THE WORLD THAT WAS

By

Philip G. Young

Rainbow's End Company
354 Golden Grove Road
Baden, PA 15005

Library of Congress Catalog Card Number: 92-64390

ISBN: 1-880451-03-4

DEDICATION

To Lael, my brother, whose keen mind and total scientific honesty first interested me in the science of the beginning.

Edited by:
Wayne P. Brumagin

Cover Design by Susan E. Campbell

"Behold, I will do a new thing; now it shall spring forth; shall
ye not know it?" *Isaiah 43:19*

TABLE OF CONTENTS

CHAPTER ONE

Bobby and Sally were waiting to see the principal when the cloakroom walls around them began to dissolve. One moment the walls were there and solid looking. The next moment they grew increasingly fuzzy and began to fade. Then they were gone. In fact, the floor was also gone, and Bobby found himself standing in a large open space. The air was heavy and damp and he felt weighted down as if he were under water. The sky faded away into a gray mist and, though it was light, no sun could be seen. Yet there was no sense of depression in that grayness for the air smelled almost spicy, rich with a deep earthy aroma.

Gazing off into the distance, Bobby saw rich black soil but no plants. He felt slightly dizzy and wondered if the rapid trip to this strange place were to blame. He felt as though he were too tall. And because the ground was so far below, it seemed as if he were looking at it from an upstairs window. Gradually, he came to realize that his head really was much higher above the ground. He looked at his feet and saw, not shoes and socks, but a velvety dark green body ending in clawed feet. Seeing a long tail stretched out behind, made him almost afraid to look at the rest of his body. UGH! No wonder he was dizzy -- his body had become that of a Tyrannosaurus Rex. His head was at least nine feet above the ground. Gaining courage, he studied his body. It did not look like any of the pictures he had seen in museums . . .

It started out as an ordinary day, but that quickly changed. A hit and run snow storm, the night before, had trimmed the trees with a layer of white. Now, as the sun began to peek over the horizon, the storm clouds had disappeared, leaving only the clear blue sky. Not even a single cloud marred the expanse of blue.

Bobby crawled out of his warm bed five minutes earlier than usual to avoid having to rush to catch the school bus. Dressing quickly, he went downstairs to the kitchen to fix his breakfast. He knew that his parents had already left for work. Every morning before leaving, his mom would quietly sneak into his room, kiss him on the forehead, and set his alarm clock so he wouldn't be late for school. He didn't want to skip breakfast because he knew it would upset her. She believed that a good breakfast is what sets the tone for the whole day. If he immediately got up when his alarm clock went off, rather than lying in bed for a few extra minutes, he found he had plenty of time to follow his mom's advice to eat something nutritious. She refused to buy sugar-coated cereals, proclaiming too much sugar wasn't good for people. Her favorite cereal was cooked oats with fruit, but it certainly wasn't Bobby's. This morning he decided to have a bowl of bran flakes with a banana sliced on top. He found he even had time to wash his dishes and put them away before grabbing his books and heading for the door.

In spite of the cold, his lightweight jacket kept him reasonably warm. Only about two inches of snow had fallen, so the three-block walk to his bus stop did not take any more time than usual. In fact, because of the snow, he arrived there a full five minutes early. This was unusual. Normally, he did not arrive at the corner until seconds before the bus pulled into sight.

He had only lived in this town for about three months which made him the new kid on the block. He was tall, skinny, and his feet seemed to grow faster than the rest of his body. While waiting for the bus, he stood apart from the other children who were talking to their friends. Quietly, he shifted his weight, uncomfortably, from one foot to the other. Reaching up, he ran his hand through his hair and glanced away from the other children as if preoccupied with his thoughts.

After the first day of school, he intentionally timed his last-minute arrivals at the bus stop so he would not have to join, or talk with, the other children. Today, as usual, they all ignored him except for Sally, who always spoke, even if it were only a cheerful, "Good morning." This morning as she approached, he noticed she was, as always, neatly dressed. "Hi, Bobby. Isn't it beautiful! I really love the snow."

Grudgingly, he answered, "So do I. It's fascinating how each snowflake has a shape of its own and is different from any other snowflake! Last night, I looked at some through my microscope." Then, as if he had said too much, he turned away.

Sally was undaunted by his behavior. "I'd love to see how a snowflake looks under a microscope. The next time it snows, will you show me?"

"Well . . . maybe," Bobby mumbled.

"Why don't you try to be more friendly? Why, you're not even friendly with the boys."

"That's not true. I'm not unfriendly," he protested. "It's just . . . It's just . . ." His voice trailed off and it was several moments before he could continue. "It's just that my family has moved around so much. It seems that every time I make friends, my parents decide to move and I have to start all over again. It's difficult for me to make new friends because it seems I like different things than they do -- things like history and science instead of baseball and bikes."

"Then you should try even harder to be friendly. Try it. It's not hard to do."

When the bus stopped, in an effort to end the conversation, Bobby hurried to find a seat by himself. Before sitting down, he made sure Sally was already seated with one of her friends. He did not want to take a chance that she might sit next to him and continue the conversation. During the ten minute ride to school, his thoughts drifted. *Should I try to play baseball with the boys even though I don't enjoy it?* He knew, if he practiced hard, that he could play as well as they did. But there were so many other more interesting things to do than playing ball. *I wish I had one good friend here at school I could talk with,* he thought. Once they arrived at the school, Bobby pushed his way to get off with the rest of the children.

As Sally left the bus, she got in the last word. "Bobby, think about what I said. Try to be more friendly."

The school building was over a hundred years old and its long narrow hallways and high ceilings gave him a sense of history. He was fascinated by old buildings such as this one -- by the many interesting nooks and crannies. Usually, as he walked to his sixth grade class, he would take his time and gaze around, but today he quickly went to his class and slunk into his back row seat.

He opened his science book, hoping that it might contain information that would tell him how he could get a clearer image on his microscope. But, he found it difficult to concentrate. It was almost as though he were in his after-lunch English class, yawning and fidgeting as he struggled to stay awake. Glancing out the window at a giant oak tree in the school yard, he noticed several early-spring robins perched on a branch, chirping as if there were no snow on the ground and they didn't have a care in the world. Standing up, he walked to the window and watched them until class began.

Bobby liked his first class -- math. He was usually the first student to finish the assigned problems, and often the teacher would call on him to complete the more difficult ones on the blackboard. Today, however, his thoughts turned to his dad's new business which was so time-consuming that he didn't seem to have time left for him. For the past two weekends, his father had promised to take him to the planetarium, but each time he'd cancelled because of important business deals. They were supposed to go this weekend and Bobby was looking forward to being with his dad. But, he was afraid that, once again, some pressing business deal would interfere.

Suddenly, he realized the teacher had called on him and he had no idea what she had asked. "I'm sorry, Miss Little. I didn't hear you."

"Bobby, where is your mind this morning? I don't think you've heard a thing I've said in the last five minutes. Are you feeling okay?"

"Yes! I'm fine!"

"Then quit daydreaming and pay attention. I asked you to do problem number five, on page 103, on the blackboard."

Slowly, getting up from his desk, he tripped over his feet, causing a series of snickers to follow as he walked to the blackboard. The math problem was easy but he did something that, for him, was very unusual -- made a careless mistake in addition. Again, he heard his classmates snicker. He was so embarrassed he wanted to run from the classroom and go home where they couldn't stare or laugh at him. But, he didn't, because he knew it would upset his dad, and he knew his dad would not let him get away with it. Finally, he muddled through to the right answer and returned to his seat.

In spite of what had happened, during the next class, his mind again began to wander. Apparently, it was going to be one of those days when nothing seems to go right. With a jerk, he turned his attention back to the classroom and saw that the teacher was looking at him sharply. He wondered if he had missed something important. Somehow, he made it through the rest of the morning but, after lunch, found his ability to concentrate was even worse. He began thinking about church and didn't know why -- his parents only went on Easter Sunday and Christmas. And, since moving here, they had never attended. A phrase he once heard in a sermon kept running through his mind. It was what Pilate said to Jesus -- *"What is truth?"*

How can a person know for sure something is true? As he pondered this question, his mind tuned out the teacher's words and the class. *What is truth? . . . What is truth? . . . What is truth? . . .* The words echoed over and over in his mind. The teacher's sharp voice snapped him back to reality. "Bobby, you didn't even hear me talking to you! And what are you mumbling about truth? This is the second time today you've failed to pay attention. That's not like you. You've left me no choice. Report to Mr. Meed in the principal's office and tell him about your behavior. Sally, will you please escort him there and stay with him until he sees Mr. Meed?"

Once again, Bobby was embarrassed and wished he could become invisible. *Did he actually say, out loud, what he had been thinking?* As they left the class, Sally asked, "What's wrong, didn't you sleep last night? You're not on drugs are you?" Her comment brought more laughter and didn't help him feel any better about himself.

"Of course not! I'm not that stupid!" he crossly replied.

When they arrived, Mr. Meed was busy seeing someone and they were asked to wait in an old cloakroom that had recently been remodeled into a waiting room. Bobby was grateful that, ever since leaving the classroom, Sally had remained silent. Trying to make up for his angry reply, he said, "This sure has been a strange day. This morning, when I woke, my mind was clear and I was alert. But, for some reason, ever since arriving at school, I feel as if I've been walking around in a dream."

"So, when you choose to be nice, you can be!" Looking around, she continued, "Isn't this the strangest waiting room! Whenever I'm in this room, I feel as if I should be wearing old-fashioned clothes. You know, perhaps a hooped skirt or a bonnet."

Bobby agreed with her. The room was long and narrow with a scattering of coathooks along the dark oak walls. But it was not the appearance that made the room so strange. He had the feeling that someone he couldn't see was watching them. It seemed as if the room itself was watching and listening. "I hope we don't have to wait very long."

"I wouldn't care if Mr. Meed completely forgets we're here. This room may be strange but it's also kind of dreamy. I wouldn't mind sitting here all day long until school is dismissed."

"I'm not sure if I'd enjoy the kind of dreams this room might give me."

Suddenly they heard a voice say, "So you're the boy who wants to know what the truth is." At first Bobby thought it was Mr. Meed speaking, but a quick glance showed that his door was still tightly closed. Looking around the room, Bobby didn't see anyone; the room itself seemed unchanged. The voice was rich, crystal clear, and had a tinkling sound, similar to a bell. It didn't sound like a man's voice, and yet, it didn't sound like a woman's voice either. As he looked around the room, he noticed it was getting brighter and brighter. Glancing at Sally, he saw her eyes were open wide with astonishment. Then he noticed what appeared to be a bright spot of light on the wall across the room, just above the coathooks. As they watched, the spot grew larger, and again they heard the strange musical voice. "It's too much bother for me to materialize. Yes! Yes! It is! Besides, we're not going to stay long and, if I materialize, you might not like how I look. By the way, my friends call me 'Gabby.' I bet you can't guess why. Yes! I do! Let's see! I know there's something very important I'm supposed to tell you... Oh! Yes! Now I remember! The best way of finding the truth is to see it. That's what I've always said. Yes! Yes! I have! You need to see it. That won't be too difficult when you're with someone like me. Let's see! Where do I begin? I should think that the proper place for me to start is at the very beginning. Yes! A very good idea! Start at the beginning." The words flowed on and on in a steady musical stream. "At first, you may find everything in the *Land of the Beginning* a bit strange but, if you relax and don't worry, you should enjoy yourselves."

If we decide to go with this Gabby character, I'm not sure we'll ever get a chance to speak, Bobby thought.

"Oh! Dear!" The voice continued, "I haven't explained to you what this is all about, have I? I keep getting ahead of myself! Yes! I do! I'm not very good at explaining! No! I'm not! It's so hard to find out about truth in today's schools. Over the years, men have gained much knowledge in many subjects, and yet, along the way, it appears they've lost wisdom and truth and forgotten where to find them.

"Bobby, when we heard you ask, 'What is truth?' our highest council met and made a decision to show you and your friend Sally what the truth is. It is our hope that perhaps, someday, you will share what you learn with others. Yes! It is! But, I still haven't explained it, have I? I've been sent here to take you on a long journey back to the Land of the Beginning so you can see how things really happened. I'm to be your guide. Oh! Dear me! I'm sure I must have forgotten something important. I usually do! Yes! I do! If I talk fast, sometimes I can remember everything I'm supposed to say before I forget. I do try! Yes! I do!"

After a long pause he continued. "Oh! Yes! How did I forget that? There are only two people in the Land of the Beginning -- Adam and Eve. We can't go there as people. Oh! Dear me! No! You will go as young dinosaurs. To be exact, each of you will be a Tyrannosaurus Rex. These days the Tyrannosauruses have a bad reputation that is totally undeserved. Actually, they are extremely intelligent and friendly. Yes! Yes! They are! So that the transformation won't be too much of a shock for you, they sent me to be your guide. I'm also a Tyrannosaurus. Yes! I am!"

It seemed to Bobby that Gabby was talking faster and faster. "There! I think I've covered everything. Oh! Yes! One more thing! In the Land of the Beginning, be careful what you say. At first, it won't be important because you'll be with me; but, later, it will be very important. You are going with me to see the truth."

While Gabby had been speaking, the bright light remained the same, but now it suddenly began to enlarge and grow brighter and brighter.

CHAPTER TWO

Bobby wondered what would happen when Mr. Meed, the principal, came for them and found they were gone. Looking around, he noticed two other Tyrannosauruses standing near him. At first he had been so absorbed in, and fascinated by his new body and surroundings, he hadn't noticed them. By studying the other Tyrannosauruses, he could visualize his own shape much better. One was slightly smaller than he and the other quite a bit larger. The smaller one was turquoise-blue in color with a single yellow ring around its neck. It had a healthy, well-rounded appearance and did not look a bit fierce. The larger one had bright colored bands of blue, green, yellow, and red which started at the tip of its nose and ran to the tip of its tail. "Well now, how do you like it here?" the larger animal asked. The voice was bell-like, crystal-clear, and sounded just like Gabby. "Never would have been able to materialize in that tiny closet. Oh! My! No! Way too crowded! Would have crushed you both!"

"This place doesn't look very special to me," the turquoise Tyrannosaurus said in a voice that sounded a lot like Sally's, but was pitched just a bit lower. "Bobby, I tried to be your friend and look where it's gotten me -- in the mud! Thank goodness, I'm no longer wearing my dress. But, I do think my blue coat is prettier than your green one. At least, I'm glad we're no longer in that spooky waiting room." Then, apparently remembering that earlier she had called it *charming,* she explained, "I was starting to feel crowded, like being in a closet."

"Don't really expect you to like it here yet," Gabby said. "We almost arrived too soon. Yes! We did! Close your eyes and rest for a minute. When I first materialize, my head always spins and I suspect yours are spinning, too. Yes! I do! After all, we've traveled a long way."

The children followed Gabby's advice. Bobby had only closed his eyes for a moment when he felt a warm spring-like breeze blow gently across his face, bringing with it the delicate fragrance of flowers. Opening his eyes, he saw that Gabby and Sally were standing nearby in what appeared to be a lush meadow alive with brilliant flowers. Perhaps it was the clean, clear air in the Land of the Beginning that made the grass seem greener than any he had ever seen before. And the colors in the flowers: the reds, blues, purples, yellows, and violets were so alive that it seemed as if he had stepped out of the dull dead colors of a painting and into the bright live colors of real life. The sky, although it remained gray, also seemed warmer.

"Oh, it's so beautiful here!" Sally exclaimed. "I've never seen such colors -- it's like a rainbow!"

"Are the colors different, or is it our eyes that are seeing things differently?" Bobby asked. Even his former friends from Dayton, had told him that he sometimes sounded too smart for his own good.

"No! You'd see the colors the same way even if you were still in your human bodies. Yes! Yes! You would! People just don't realize the effects of sin." The last words were spoken so softly that the children barely heard them. "Believe me, the colors are real. Yes! Yes! They are! Sally, are you feeling better about being here? Are you more comfortable?"

"I -- I think I like it here. Are we in the Garden of Eden?" She recalled how, when she was younger, her family had gone to church every Sunday; but then, about two years ago, a new pastor was assigned and they stopped going. But she'd learned about Adam and Eve in Sunday School and knew that they belonged to the time of the beginning.

Oh! Dear me! No! This is just the beginning of the beginning. We're at the beginning of the new world. You need time to adjust to this new world before you get to see the Garden. Yes! You do! The Garden isn't yet, and it's a long way from here, but not too far for a Tyrannosaurus."

"Gabby, how old is the world we see then," Bobby wanted to know. "Are we truly at the very beginning?"

"Oh! Dear me! With me being so poor in math, that's a difficult question to answer. I'm afraid I'll get things all mixed up. Let me think! Yes! Yes! That's it! The heavens, with the mist above, were sorted out yesterday and the ocean was formed earlier today -- you'll get to see it sometime. Yes! Yes! You will! We arrived just minutes before the trees and plants were brought forth. Wouldn't have done to arrive before there was something to eat. Oh! Dear me! No! Came as soon as it was practical. So how old do you think the earth is? One day? Two days? Three days? Take your choice. The best I can tell you is we're at the beginning, and the earth, if I've counted right, is three days old."

"I could never tell that it was the beginning," Sally commented. "The grass looks the same as back home -- only fresher. And those trees across the meadow look quite old. Why, some are as big as the one my playhouse is in!"

"I don't see any dead branches," Bobby exclaimed.

"Oh! Dear me! No! We're in a time before death. Oh! No! You won't find anything dead here. Not even a tiny branch."

Bobby responded to this with another question. "What about eating then? Isn't a plant dead when you eat it?"

"A plant isn't alive the same way that an animal is. Oh! No! A plant is a food-making factory that God created to be eaten. There's a difference between the world you live in and that of the Land of the Beginning. Here nothing is wasted! When fruit ripens, it doesn't fall to the ground and rot. It stays on the tree until it is eaten by an animal that needs it for food. In that way everything is being used as God meant it to be. Yes!"

"So the trees store their own fruit," Bobby remarked. "Neat! No need for refrigerators."

"Speaking of food," Sally joined in, "I'm hungry. How will I know what's good to eat? Do I just eat what looks and smells good? I'm sure some of the plants must be poisonous. If they're poisonous, do they look or smell differently? I'm confused! The only place I've ever seen food was in the supermarket and our refrigerator. Why, I've never even been on a farm."

"In the beginning everything is good to eat. Yes! Yes! It is! I told you there is no waste. Everything is good, but some things are better. At other times, other things are better. Come! See!" He ambled off toward the nearby trees, talking to himself as he went.

"Look it's an apple grove!" Bobby exclaimed as they drew near. "But not all of the trees look the same. Gabby, why are some different than the others?"

"Many people in your day, even if they believe in the beginning, seem to think things are limited and simple. Yes! They do! But that isn't true. There's just as much variety now as in your day. In fact, there's even more variety, since many of the plants that exist here became extinct and no longer exist in your day. Here they all grow in abundance. Oh! I do love apples! Yes! I do! Look over there -- Johnathans, Baldwins, and Red and Golden Delicious. And over there -- Roman Beauty, Ben Davis and McIntosh. And back a couple of rows, Rhode Island Greening, Northern Spy, Winesap and many, many more. Oh! I do love apples!"

Each apple was perfectly ripe without a spot on it. For the next few minutes the only sound heard was the crisp, crunchy sound of apples being eaten. Even Gabby was quiet. The apples were larger, crispier, and more refreshing than any Bobby or Sally had ever tasted.

After their appetites were satisfied, Bobby asked, "Gabby, you seem to know so much. How old are you?"

"Well now! You do ask the most difficult questions. Yes! You do! The best I can say is I'm from near the beginning. But then, I've lived in a place where time isn't the same as in your world. But that's not important. No! No! It isn't! What is important Bobby, is for you to concentrate on seeing the truth at the beginning of your own world."

"But, are you really a Tyrannosaurus?"

"That's also unimportant! I'm just as much a Tyrannosaurus as you are. What's important is for you and Sally to understand something about the flow of time. Oh! Yes! Yes! Very important! How old do you think I look? That's a more important question."

"I'm good at guessing ages," Sally replied. "But I've never seen a real live dinosaur before, and have no idea how long a dinosaur can live. So, how can I guess your age?"

"Good! Good! Now you're starting to think."

"You must be an adult Tyrannosaurus," Bobby surmised, or, at least be older, because you're bigger than we are."

"You're right again! Yes! You are! A Tyrannosaurus is born with one ring; then, starting at age thirteen, adds a new ring about every five years! You each have a single ring while I have many. So, if you study and gain knowledge of Tyrannosauruses, you will find that your bodies couldn't have hatched more than twelve years ago. My body looks as if it's at least three-hundred earth years old. Yes! It does!"

"I'm confused," Sally said. "How can things look old if it's the beginning? Shouldn't everything look brand new? The trees look old; you look old. In the beginning shouldn't everything look young?"

"One cannot create something without giving it an appearance of being old. No! They can't! That's one of the things I brought you here to see -- one of the reasons why I brought you to the very beginning -- to the start of your journey to see the truth. That's why it's important to look around. Yes! Nothing here, other than you and I, is more than three days old. In your world an apple tree takes sixty years to grow to the size of these trees. So -- your mind -- your experience -- tells you these trees must also be at least sixty years old."

"I haven't seen the sun," Bobby said. "But it's still as bright as it is back home on a cloudy day."

"The Creator won't set the sun up to rule over the earth until tomorrow. No! He won't! Not until tomorrow! For now, Bobby, you see light only."

"I would never have guessed the earth is older than the sun. Some scientists claim the sun is about three billion years old."

"That's because events in the life of a star take a long time; it's a star's nature to look old. Oh! Dear me! Yes! A young star would be too hot to allow life to exist. Yes! And it would be so big that it would completely cover the earth. Yes! Yes! So tomorrow The Creator will place a medium-aged sun in the sky, a sun which will be just the right size for earth."

Sally sounded puzzled. "Why did God make the earth look so old? My teachers at school say that it's very old."

"That's because men don't listen to what God, The Creator, has told them. No! No! They don't! The only way to know the truth is to listen to His Word. He has told them in His Word that the earth is very young."

Sally was persistent, "I still don't understand why the earth looks old!"

"That's one of the things I want you to discover. Yes! Yes! It is! But don't make the mistake of thinking you can discover everything. Some things will have to be revealed to you. Yes! They will! Remember, you have seen very little of this world of the time of the beginning. Later, after you have been here longer, you'll understand more. Tell me, what do you think of this world so far?"

"It's beautiful," Sally said. "I just wish there were more people my age here so I wouldn't get lonely. It there were, I think I'd like to stay!"

"Oh! Dear me! No! It's not possible for you to stay. No! It isn't! But, I expect you will grow to like this world more and more because it's The Creator's unspoiled handiwork. You are catching a small glimpse of what He wanted this world to be."

Bobby was pretty sure he knew the answer to his next question. "If we study the world He made, will it help us to find out more about The Creator?"

"Yes! Yes! You're on the right track! Keep thinking! That shouldn't be too difficult for an intelligent boy like you. It's much easier when you see the world at the beginning, before it's been scarred by sin. Yes! Yes! It is!"

"God, The Creator, must be beautiful for His world is so beautiful," Sally said. "I love beautiful things. Does the world look old because God is old?"

Gabby bobbed his head three times and almost did a little dance. "Right! Right!" he cried. "The world looks old because God is eternal and has always existed. Now you're beginning to see a small part of the truth. Yes! You are!"

"The flowers don't look old!"

"That's another part of the truth, Bobby. Yes! Yes! It is! The flowers are young. They're telling you that the earth is young."

Bobby thought for a moment and then said, "Does that mean when science discovers something which makes the earth appear to be young, God is telling us something -- that the earth is young? And, when nature appears to be old, is God telling us something about Himself -- that He is eternal -- that He lives forever?"

"Yes! Yes! I couldn't have said it better. But come! Tomorrow is going to be a long day; the light is fading, and we need to find a place to sleep. You two are accustomed to sleeping in houses and, at first, it may feel uncomfortable for you to sleep outside." He lumbered off to the West where the sky was beginning to grow dark. The children had to hurry to keep up with him.

CHAPTER THREE

Bobby awoke with a start, trying to remember where he was. It was early morning. Even though he was not in his own bed, he was certainly comfortable. It felt as if he were resting on a soft cushion of feathery down. Looking around he saw that he was lying on a thick, soft layer of moss under a dark green canopy of huge leaves. His green Tyrannosaurus' limbs were speckled by light filtering down through the leaves. Then he remembered the extraordinary dream-like events of the day before.

Gabby and Sally were still sleeping so he quietly stood and walked out into the meadow. Heavy dew lay on the grass, twinkling like a thousand tiny pearls of light. Something was different and, for a moment, he was puzzled as to what had changed. Then it dawned on him -- it was the sun. There it was; a large orange-yellow ball, appearing for the first time above the horizon. No longer was the sky gray, but a brilliant blue. It seemed bluer, cleaner and had more depth than any sky he had ever seen. Yes, that was it. It seemed deeper -- as if it were higher above the earth and reached further into the heavens than the sky back home.

He heard a soft swooshing noise in the grass next to him. Sally was awake and had come to stand beside him. "Oh, it's so beautiful," she sighed. "I thought it was beautiful yesterday, but now ... I don't think I'm ever going to want to leave. I wish I could take all this -- the sun, sky and meadow -- everything back with me to share with my friends."

It was not just the sky and the sun. The meadow itself seemed brighter as if it, too, had taken on new, stronger colors. Bobby started to jump up and down to see how high he could jump. Sally began to run in circles, chasing her tail. Finally they collapsed in a helpless heap of laughter. What a wonderful, beautiful world God had created! From somewhere the refrain, *"This is the day that the Lord has made. I will rejoice and be glad in it,"* entered Bobby's mind. He stood quietly, looking out over the beauty of the meadow, wondering what additional marvels lay beyond his sight.

A few moments later Gabby joined them. "Come along now! Can't stand gazing around forever even though the sights are new to you. We have lots to do. Yes! Yes! We do! But first it's time for us to eat. Time for you to discover why a Tyrannosaurus has teeth." Gabby began walking toward the trees which lined the meadow.

The mention of food made the children realize how hungry they were. In fact, they were famished. So, although they felt reluctant to leave such a wonderful place, they followed where he led them.

They plunged through a thick fringe of brush at the meadow's edge and found they were in what looked like a tropical rain forest. Huge vine-draped trees towered above. Here and there, streams of sunlight filtered down like spotlights through the leaves overhead. The forest floor was covered with a dark green blanket of moss and ferns. White, blue, purple and gold orchids were everywhere. It was so quiet they could almost feel the stillness. Sally walked slowly as she gazed around, finally coming to a complete stop. "I don't know which is more beautiful -- the meadow -- or here. What a great place this would be to practice my violin."

"Oh! My! Yes! I agree with you. The forest does seem like a giant cathedral with all its beauty shouting praise to God, the Creator. Yes!"

"It's so quiet. Just the trees, flowers and us. I haven't seen or heard a bird or insect since entering the forest," Bobby said.

"That's because this is only the fourth day. Yes! The birds and insects haven't been created yet. No! No! Not yet!"

"How can we be here, then?" Bobby asked. "How is it possible for us to be here before creation is finished?"

"We're here because the earth is ready for life. Oh! Yes! Of course! And, we're here because you need to see the truth -- that God created the world out of nothing. You need to understand that God is God and not just a part of nature. God is beyond nature, greater than nature. Yes! He is! It's important that you know that everything you see here was made in a very short time. Yes! Then you will also understand that nature didn't create itself as some people claim. No sense in those ideas! No! None at all! Come straight from the *'Evil one,'* they do! I'll tell you more about him later. But, come along now! We're almost at our destination."

The beauty and quietness of the forest gripped them as they reluctantly followed Gabby further under the tree canopy. "It's so quiet and beautiful that one almost has to think about God. Just think, two days ago these trees and flowers weren't even here. God must surely be great to create these things," Bobby said.

"I was always so busy with my friends that I never really took time to think about God," Sally added thoughtfully. "I think most people are like me, so busy that even when they do slow down, it's to think about what they're going to do, and not about God. My friends never mention God. We talk about what games to play, what boys we like -- you know, things like that."

"Oh! Yes! Yes! I think you're beginning to see," Gabby said with satisfaction. "Some of our most important seeing is not done with the eyes." Suddenly he stopped. "We're here!" He was standing next to a large tree weighted down with red, melon-sized fruit. "Come! Eat!" he invited them.

Bobby discovered if he sat back on his haunches, he could use the long toes on his front feet like fingers. At first it was awkward, but a Tyrannosaurus has excellent coordination so it was not long before he was entirely comfortable using his front feet. With practice he found he could do everything he used to do with his hands. Following Gabby's example, he reached up and twisted a piece of fruit off from a branch. As he studied it, he realized he had no idea what kind of fruit it was. Never before had he seen anything like it. Taking his first bite, he found the reddish flesh of the fruit was encased in a thick, fibrous pod which required the full power of his jaws to break. After swallowing, he decided that biting through the thick pod was worth the effort. The fruit was rich and creamy -- delicious! Bobby tried to remember what the taste reminded him of. Finally he decided it tasted similar to Custard Apple -- a tropical fruit he had eaten only once. But this fruit did not have the multiple seeds of a Custard Apple; it had only a single medium-sized seed in the center.

"Shouldn't we wash our food before eating?" Sally asked, joining them. "And, aren't we going to get our faces dirty eating something that big?" She liked to stay clean.

"You don't have to worry about germs here. Oh! No! You don't!" Gabby reassured her. "Eat and enjoy."

Still, Sally hesitated. Then hunger overcame her desire for neatness and she, too, twisted a piece of fruit from a branch. Biting into it, a smile spread across her face.

"Why does the fruit have such a thick pod?" Bobby asked.

"One reason is the pod helps to keep it fresh. If the pod were thinner, it would lose much of its taste. Yes! You can see how rich the fruit is. If the pod were easy to open, the smaller animals might eat too much. Yes! They would!"

"I can understand why they would want to eat too much," Sally commented. "I could keep on eating and eating and eating."

But she was wrong because suddenly they were full, and realized it would not be right to eat more. Bobby gave a contented sigh. "I'm not hungry anymore, but I sure am thirsty."

"There's a stream not far away," Gabby responded. "We're going there next."

They did., The water was pure, sweet and refreshing. They drank their fill. After satisfying their thirst, they returned to stand under the warm rays of the gentle sun. Sally asked, "In the beginning did the animals do anything useful? Or did they just eat, sleep and enjoy themselves?"

"God gave every animal a purpose. Yes! Yes! He did! The fruit we ate is an example. Many animals can't open the strong pods because their teeth are weak. So we Tyrannosauruses, with our strong jaws and large claws, open more fruit than we will eat so they can feed on what we leave. Yes! They can! As you learn more, you'll find that in the Land of the Beginning everyone cooperates for the good of others -- nature is in perfect balance. You'll see more of this later. Yes! Yes! You will!"

"Do things change here?" Bobby asked. "Or does everything remain the same?"

"Oh! Dear me! Of course things change. Change is what the fourth day is all about. Yes! It is! God said, '*Let there be lights in the expanse of the heavens to divide the day from the night; and let them be for signs and for seasons and for days and for years.*' You can read about what He said in the Book He gave to men -- His Bible. That's what the fourth day is for -- to add variety to His creation. God has given His creation both permanence and change. Yes! He has!"

"I've never read the Bible," Sally admitted. "Though I did hear it read at church sometimes. And I think we have one at home -- on our living room shelf."

"The reason so few people know and love the truth in your day is that they don't study about God's truth in the Bible. If they did, you wouldn't be making this trip to see the truth. No! You wouldn't! It's important you make this trip while you're young. Yes! When people get old and set in their ways, it's difficult for them to accept change. They like permanence and familiar things. Yes! They do! I'm sure your parents have a favorite food or chair. But, if things always stayed the same, I bet they'd be bored. Yes! They would! That's why God gives us change. Every day is different with light during the day and darkness at night. And then He adds the seasons: summer, fall, winter and spring. Each season following the next! Yes! Yes! So there are always changes, but underlying those changes, there is permanence."

"Does God change?" Bobby asked.

"Dear me! No! Oh! No! Never!" Gabby emphatically replied. "God never changes! He's the same in your world as here in the beginning. His truth never changes. Oh! No! It never changes! That's one of the reasons why, by coming here, you can see the truth. If He changed, He wouldn't be God. And, if He did change, you couldn't trust Him because then He might not be the same God tomorrow as He is today. He might not be the same God in the beginning as He is in your day. God never changes! No! Oh! No! You can rely on every word He says!"

"What are the seasons like here in the Land of the Beginning?" Sally asked. "I hate being cold and, no matter where I am, I don't think I'd like winter."

"Some places around the equator don't have winter," Bobby piped up, "but still have seasons."

Sally shook her head. "Everything stays the same year-round in the tropics, and I don't think those are real seasons."

"In the beginning there's no rain, just dew. So there's no ice or snow. No! But there are seasons. Yes! There are! Could you imagine what the beginning was like before I brought you here? You'd have a hard time recognizing the seasons unless I pointed them out. But the world changed before the seasons truly began so there's no way I can show you now, the way they truly were at the beginning. No! I can't! Someday you may see the seasons of the world that was, but not the seasons as they would have been in the beginning. But perhaps not before you return home. Seasons here have the same beauty and wonder as in your day but little of the ugliness. No! Not the ugliness! Sally, I'm sure, will agree that the seasons are dazzlingly beautiful."

Between eating and conversation, the day passed swiftly. They ate fruit several more times. While some, such as the large red strawberries were familiar, most were unfamiliar. All were delicious. Sally tasted the strawberries, knowing that they were too small to make much of a meal for a Tyrannosaurus. They were the best tasting she had ever eaten, and she wished they were bigger. Actually they were quite large, almost the size of a peach.

The children were glad when the sun sank below the horizon and the sky became filled with brilliant stars. Bobby noticed the constellations were different and the stars didn't twinkle; instead, they gave off a steady unwinking light. This puzzled him so he questioned Gabby, "Why aren't the stars twinkling like they do back home?"

"Why do they twinkle on earth?"

"I've read it has something to do with the atmosphere but I don't really know why."

"Yes! Yes! Right again! It's the atmosphere that makes them twinkle. But here the sky is so clear they don't twinkle. You see the stars as they really are."

"I could stay up all night just looking at the stars," Sally said. "I love to stay up late."

"This is fun and maybe some night we can, but not tonight. Tomorrow we have a big journey ahead of us. Yes! Yes! A big journey!" Gabby led them out of the meadow in search of a soft, moss-carpet bed under the trees.

CHAPTER FOUR

The next morning when Bobby awoke it was still dark, though the darkness was fading fast. Through the network of leaves which formed a mat over his head, he saw stars brightly shining in the rapidly lightening sky. He wasn't sure what had awakened him since everything was quiet. Except for the deep steady breathing of Gabby and Sally, not a sound was heard. There was no wind; not a single leaf was stirring. But, inside, he felt a curious sense of urgency -- of expectancy -- that grew stronger and stronger each passing minute.

Then, faint and far away, he heard something -- a deep humming sound that grew closer and closer. Just as the sun came up, he suddenly realized that birds were singing all around him. Not just one or two, but a whole chorus. He could not identify or name the birds, but he knew in all his life he had never heard such lovely music. The whole earth seemed to tremble with joy as it was caught up in the riot of sound. It was not just the birds -- he also heard crickets happily chirping and, further away, the distant croaking of frogs as they added to the melody. "Sally! Sally! Wake up!"

"What for? I just went to sleep," Sally said in a drowsy voice.

"Get up sleepyhead, it's morning! And there's much for us to see. The animals have arrived."

And they had! Bobby saw a furry head peeking at them from behind a bush. It was a chipmunk, but a larger, sleeker chipmunk than any he had ever seen. It scampered up to them chattering and waving it's tail. "It acts like it's trying to say something," he said.

"Yes! Yes! Of course it is! It just told me it is time for me to get up," Gabby said, opening his eyes. "Every animal has its own language, though most animal languages consist of only a few words. But here, in the Land of the Beginning, some dinosaurs speak the human language and most of the other languages as well. That's one reason why we came here as Tyrannosauruses. Most animals are too limited in the sounds they can make to be able to speak human language. Yes! Yes! They are! Oh, there are a few birds that speak, but they're not intelligent enough to fully understand the language."

"What's the chipmunk saying now?" Sally asked.

"What do you think? Listen! Yes! Listen!"

"I think he's saying he's glad to see us," she answered.

"Yes! Yes! He is glad to see us! But that's not what he's saying. Listen! Closely!"

It seemed to the children that, just like a blurred picture comes into focus when you adjust the projector lens, so also did the chipmunk sounds come into focus. "Who are you? Who are you?" the chirpy voice was saying. "Isn't today a delightful day? Why don't you come play with me and join in praising my wonderful Maker?"

"Who are you?" Gabby asked in chipmunk language.

"I'm Chippy-Chip, master nut craftsman for my Lord. I know how all the nuts grow and when they taste their best -- when they've gained that deep satisfying, nutty-flavored ripeness. I know which nuts taste better after being buried in the earth and also the ones whose flavor is improved after being covered with a light layer of leaves. I am a master of nut craft. But, tell me, who are you?"

"We're Tyrannosauruses," Gabby replied. "Guardians of the knowledge of the Land of the Beginning."

Bobby asked a question. "If Chippy-Chip was just created, how come he can talk and knows so much?"

"Oh! You children do ask a lot of questions! Yes! Yes! You do! When the Lord of Creation created each creature, He gave it the knowledge to do its job, to fulfill its role. Yes! He did!" Turning to Chippy-Chip he continued, "We'd be honored to play in the meadow with you; however, we have a long journey and can't stay here to visit. I'm sure you'll find other friends and playmates in the meadow."

But Sally's wistful voice caused him to change his mind. "Gabby, it's such a beautiful day. Please, can't we stay and play?"

"Yes! Yes! I guess! All right! But only for a little while. We can't stay long or we'll miss some important things I want you to see."

As they walked from the trees to the meadow, Gabby turned and said, "We Tyrannosauruses speak most of the world's languages but some animals have words in their language that we can't pronounce. Adam, as lord under the High Lord, has been given the ability by The Creator to speak them all. Yes! Yes! He has! Soon we'll go to the Garden and find Adam so you can see the truth you came here to see. But we have to be careful." His last words were said with a sigh.

"Why? ... Why do we have to be careful?" Bobby asked. They were now in the meadow where the buzzing sounds of contented bees filled the air and large bright butterflies flitted from flower to flower. Bobby watched as Chippy-Chip chased after the butterflies, turning somersaults in the grass. "It's so peaceful I could stretch out in the sun and nap for hours."

"Be careful! Oh dear! I'm so poor at explaining!" Gabby had stopped and was sitting up on his haunches. "Perhaps this might help," he said, slipping one of his claws into a kangaroo-like pouch on his chest.

Bobby watched as Gabby took a book from his pouch. "This is the book God has given to you humans. Yes! Yes! It is!" he said, as he stopped flipping through the pages and began to read, " *And out of the ground made the Lord God to grow every tree that is pleasant to the sight, and good for food; the Tree of Life also in the midst of the Garden, and the Tree of Knowledge of Good and Evil. And the Lord God took the man and put him into the Garden of Eden to dress it and keep it. And the Lord God commanded the man saying, of every tree of the Garden, thou mayest freely eat: But of the Tree of Knowledge of Good and Evil, thou shall not eat of it, for in the day that thou eatest thereof thou shalt surely die!* "

"What does it mean?" Bobby asked.

"Oh! Dear me! I never seem to know how to explain things. Yes! I don't! I'm trying to tell you about evil -- the very real evil that walks in this land. And that's not pleasant to talk about. Not even in the best of times. No! Indeed not!"

"Are you saying that even here, in the Land of the Beginning, there is evil?"

"Bobby, you heard what I just read. I do wish I were better at explaining these things. Yes! I do!"

Sally wanted to simplify things. "Gabby, the only evil you mentioned was eating from a tree in the Garden of Eden and we're not even in the Garden yet. So why are we talking about it? Can't we just play and have fun?"

"Oh dear! I'm so bad at explaining! Yes! I am! Perhaps if I could find the right place to start..." Gabby, arms clasped behind his head, paused for nearly a minute to think; then he asked them a question, "Tell me, is the Tree of Knowledge of Good and Evil... good or evil?"

"Evil," Sally promptly replied. "Why did God put such a tree in the Garden?"

"Good!" Bobby said. "Everything made by The Creator that I've seen in the Land of the Beginning is good. So I think the Tree of Knowledge of Good and Evil must also be good."

"You're right, Bobby. Yes! Yes! You are!" Turning the pages in the book, he continued, "In His Book it is written, '*And God looked on all He had made and behold it was very good!*' "

Sally was confused. "I don't understand," she said. "How could putting evil in the middle of the Garden be good?"

"Oh! Dear me! No! He didn't place evil in the Garden. He put knowledge there -- the knowledge of both good and evil."

"Why did He do that?" Bobby asked.

"Oh, my! I hope I'm not making things too difficult. Evil is possible anywhere, even in paradise. Yes! It is! Do you honestly believe that a tree can be evil? The tree is in the Garden, not *to be* good or evil, but to teach us a lesson *about* good and evil. Oh! Dear me! I do wish I could explain better. How do you determine what is good and what is bad? Some things you just know. Yes! You do! For example, you wouldn't jump from a rooftop because you know you'd get hurt. But do you automatically know it's not good to eat a lot of fatty foods? You don't! No, you don't! In fact, fatty foods often taste better but they're still not good for you. Only a doctor, dietician, or some other knowledgeable person can tell you fat raises your cholesterol. It isn't good for you. No! No! It isn't!"

"Why didn't God create two trees: one good and one evil?" Bobby asked. "Why are good and evil both represented in the same tree?"

"Most things used for good can also be twisted and used for evil. Yes! Yes! They can! God is reminding Adam he must depend on His wisdom to ensure that something intended for good is not used for evil."

"Are you saying only God knows what's good for me?" Sally asked, trying to follow Gabby's thoughts. Then, after asking, she whirled around and began to playfully chase her tail.

"Right! Right on!" Gabby replied, not paying any attention to her antics. "Men have to learn what is evil so they can avoid it and live good lives. Yes! Yes! But all evil isn't obvious and must be identified. That's the secret of true knowledge. And that true knowledge can only come from God."

"You mean Adam wouldn't have known it was wrong to eat the fruit from this tree if God hadn't told him?"

"That's right, Bobby! Yes! Yes! And the tree is a constant reminder to Adam that if he truly wants to be a good caretaker, a good steward of the Garden, there are many things he needs to ask God. At all times he needs to check with God. Even though God never does anything evil, He is the only one who can fully understand and recognize all good and evil. Yes! Yes! Only He! As I said before, there is evil in the world of the beginning."

Slowly looking around, Bobby said, "I don't see anything evil. Everything... everything looks beautiful and good. With all the birds, bees, flowers and butterflies, it's just like paradise. It's even more beautiful than anything I could imagine in my dreams."

"I'm sure you're familiar with the rest of the story," Gabby continued as if he hadn't heard Bobby's comment. "Most men have heard the story but, unfortunately, many don't believe it. I don't like to talk about it or even think about it. But then, there are many things a person doesn't like to do, yet has to do."

"Are you talking about the Serpent?" Sally asked. "I remember the Bible says there was a serpent in the Garden."

"Yes! Yes! Of course I am! But remember, this serpent isn't like any other snake in the world. Oh! No! No! It's nothing like a snake. Oh! Dear me! No!"

"One of my friends told me the reason snakes don't have legs and crawl on their bellies is because of what happened in the Garden," Sally said. "But I thought she was joking, pulling my leg."

The word *leg*, triggered another question from Bobby. "Did snakes once have legs?" he asked.

"The truth is worse. Yes! Yes! It is! The Serpent in the Garden is a Tyrannosaurus. Oh! Dear me! Remember, when I told you Tyrannosauruses were the only animals in the Garden that could clearly speak the human language? Well, you should have guessed from that. The Serpent in the Garden is like us, a Tyrannosaurus. That's why we have to be very careful. The Evil One is here! Here at the beginning! Yes! He is!"

CHAPTER FIVE

Bobby and Sally stood staring at Gabby for at least a minute, unable to speak. Then Bobby softly said, "I don't know what kind of an enemy he is but a Tyrannosaurus with the character of a serpent sounds pretty nasty."

"You're right! Yes! Yes! There is reason for concern. In your world the serpent is the one who is behind all war, disease, and heartache. Remember though, The God of Creation is far greater than the Serpent. He's the One who has allowed you to come to the Land of the Beginning to see the truth. Yes! He's the One! Nothing can successfully challenge the fulfillment of His will. Before pride corrupted his heart, and he decided to rebel against God, it had been the duty of the Evil One to uphold mercy and justice. But enough about the Serpent! In the world that has come to be, God doesn't keep His servants from danger but; instead, accomplishes His perfect will through their lives. Yes! Yes! He does! Remember, nothing gives the Evil One more pleasure than trying to thwart God's will. At times, it may even seem that he succeeds, but it's only a temporary illusion. It lasts just for a season.

"Come! We must not linger here any longer. No! Later today, things are going to happen in the Garden that the Evil One doesn't want you to see. That's enough reason for us not to be late. So far we've traveled slowly so you could get accustomed to your new bodies and to allow you time to enjoy the new world. But, now we have to hurry! Yes! We do!"

Bobby was apprehensive. "If the Serpent is a Tyrannosaurus and looks like us, is it possible I might confuse him with you? Could I wake up some morning and find I'm following him instead of you? The very thought is enough to give me nightmares. How will I be able to tell you apart?"

"Every Tyrannosaurus is different," Gabby said stretching his multi-ringed, brilliantly colored body upward. "Oh! Dear me! Yes! Yes! They are! I'm much too plain looking to be mistaken for the Serpent. Yes! I am! One of the Serpent's names is 'Shining One.' He's called that because he's decked out in royal colors -- gold and purple rings from head to toe. But that's not all; each gold ring contains a different kind of precious stone -- red rubies, green jades, blue sapphires. And the gold ring at the very top of his head is filled with glittering diamonds. Oh! No! I'm much too plain."

"Does the Evil One have helpers?"

"Oh! Dear me! Yes! But not as many as God."

"What do his helpers look like? Bobby asked. "Are they dangerous, too?"

"Most of his helpers aren't from this world, and you can't see them because, just like God's messengers, they're invisible. But, don't worry! No! No! Don't worry! We'll have help if the need arises. Because this world is so new, the Evil One hasn't had much time or opportunity to corrupt the animals. But later it will be different. After the fall, the wolves, ravens, dragons and others will follow him and become his creatures. Yes! But, I'm getting ahead of myself. This is some of the truth you've come to see. Right now the Evil One has no friends to help him, but he still may try to attack your mind and heart with doubt and fear. All fear and discouragement comes from him. Yes! Yes! It does! They are two of his favorite weapons he uses to reach you but -- they aren't his only weapons!"

"Can I go home? Sally said, snuggling close to Gabby. "I've always been afraid of snakes, and with a super snake on the loose, I'm terrified!"

"Sally, didn't you hear Gabby tell us the Serpent lives in our world, too. Returning home won't protect you from him."

"But I feel more exposed here where everything is so open," Sally explained. "There's no houses -- only meadows, trees, and open space."

"Now isn't the time to be thinking such thoughts," Bobby told her. "It sounds like the Serpent has already put some of that doubt and fear into your mind and heart. So far everything we've experienced here has been marvelous. I think what we're learning is worth the danger. And I'm sure that in the days ahead, the truths we learn will be just as important. A God who can create the things we've seen, surely, is also capable of taking care of us!"

"Yes! Yes! You're right! God will take care of and protect us! Hurry! There's no time to waste. We have to get to the Garden. Yes! We do! We've already spent too much time talking. It isn't far. Just over those hills! Hurry! It isn't going to be easy getting there."

Never pausing to look back to see if the children were following, Gabby, with huge strides, walked across the meadow toward the distant hills. He didn't look back. He knew they were behind him by the swishing noise their large tails made in the deep meadow grass.

For half an hour they walked through the meadow and never spoke. Finally Gabby stopped near the top of the ridge of hills. Turning, he gazed at Sally and said, "Don't worry! When danger comes, you'll find you'll have the courage to face it. The strangeness and the newness of this world has made you homesick. But, don't worry; it will pass. Yes! Yes! It will!"

They noticed the bottom of the hills were obscured by a heavy mist, and beyond the mist was, what appeared to be, a long valley awash in a kaleidoscope of colors. Pointing at the colors, Gabby said, "That's the edge of the Garden. We're almost there! Yes! Yes! We are! But, we have to hurry. Some of the most difficult travel is still ahead."

Ten minutes more brought them to the edge of the mist. As they approached, a gentle breeze caught the mist and momentarily blew it away, revealing a jumbled pile of jagged rocks and many pools of steaming water. Gabby began to share information with them. "This area of the Garden is edged by hot springs. It's called, 'The Uncertain Land,' because mist frequently hides the ground, making footing treacherous and uncertain. Yes! It does! We could avoid this area and enter the Garden another way but it would take us another day and we don't have the time. So we'll risk walking through this Uncertain Land. We'll be safe if we're careful and watch where we step. When mist obscures our vision and we can't see where to step, we'll have to be patient and not rush. Here we go! Follow me, closely! And, if you can't see where I place my feet, tell me right away."

After taking a half dozen steps, it seemed as if they had entered another world. It was eerie. The mist was so thick that they could no longer see the sky. They were in a gray, damp world with heavy, warm air that smelled faintly like sulphur. The mist totally blotted out the sky but it wasn't thick enough to obscure their vision. However, approaching some of the large steaming pools, it became so moist that water ran down their foreheads into their eyes. This almost blinded them and made it extremely difficult for them to stay on the path. When this happened, Gabby encouraged them, "It's okay! Yes! Yes! It is! Follow me! Follow my steps! Don't step where you can't see."

The mist was scary, but the sounds they heard all around them were even more frightening. It wasn't just the low, rumbling, bubbling noise of hot steam popping up through the pools that scared them -- it was the low pitched moaning sounds which seemed to surround them, and the heavy plodding sounds of footsteps which seemed to be following them.

"How long will it be before we get out of here?" Bobby asked. "I'm scared!"

"Me, too!" Sally chimed in.

"Most of the noise you hear is caused by the mud. As it expands, it makes moaning sounds. Yes! It does! Don't be afraid! It shouldn't take us more than another half hour to get out of here. These springs are important. When the weather is cool, they warm the Garden.

Yes! They do! And at night the mist, floating over the Garden, waters the plants. I promise you the Garden is truly beautiful. Have patience; we're almost there."

They were now past the bog. The pools were larger, hotter, and the sounds of their bubbling were sharper and crisper. Gabby stopped. The ridge they were walking on had abruptly ended in a jumble of boulders. From this point on, they would have to carefully pick their way between the boiling pools. They slowed their pace to a deliberate, plodding walk. Five, ten, twenty minutes rolled slowly by as they toiled onward. The children were carefully trying to place their feet exactly where Gabby placed his. Suddenly, a gust of wind blew the mist away and there was the Garden, not more than a hundred yards away. "See! We're almost there! Yes! Yes! We are!"

A wild scream sounded behind them. Startled, Sally jumped forward, crashing into Bobby, causing both of them to fall and slide feet first into one of the steaming pools. As their feet hit the bubbling hot water, they screamed in pain. Fortunately, the pool was shallow, not deep like so many. They quickly scrambled out of it, but not before badly burning their feet. Sally insisted that just before falling she had seen a large face loom out of the mist -- the face of a Tyrannosaurus -- gold and purple, with twinkling points of light as if covered with gems. The wild scream they heard came from the Evil One himself! Oddly enough, this incident didn't frighten them. It just made them angry.

Gabby urged them forward. "Hurry! Hurry up! There are streams of cool water in the Garden. The water will help your feet. Yes! Yes! It will be another delay, but it can't be helped. Hurry! Hurry now!"

With every step their burned feet hurt more and more until finally each step was agonizing. Sally whimpered while Bobby tried bravely not to show his pain but, eventually, the pain became too great and he, too, began to moan.

Finally, they were out of the mist and at the edge of the Garden. Looking around, they saw that the Garden was even better than Gabby said. They would have liked to spend some time admiring its beauty but couldn't, because their world was a world of painful feet. A shallow stream of crystal clear water was flowing a few feet away. Quickly they stepped into it and waded into its cool depths. If felt so good, so soothing to their burning feet; they expressed their feelings with grateful sighs. With every step, the stinging and burning lessened. "Golly, my pain is almost gone," Sally exclaimed with surprise. "Maybe my feet weren't burned as badly as I thought."

"Oh! No! No! Don't kid yourself! Your feet were horribly burned. Yes! They were! You're in a land that death hasn't touched. Death has no power here, so the body's power to heal is still complete. In the Land of the Beginning, injuries may cause pain but can't bring death. Here, it takes the body less than an hour to heal that which, in your world, would take weeks. In another ten minutes your burns will be completely healed with no scarring. Yes! They will! Oh! My! We've lost precious time. This is an important day for you to see and understand the truth. But," he added a moment later, "if, in the days ahead, nothing more serious than minor burns happen after an encounter with the Evil One, I will be pleased indeed!"

Bobby had watched his feet from the moment he stepped out of the steaming hot water. He noticed that the instant he walked into the cool stream they had started to heal. And now, where the blisters had been, was fresh skin! "Look, my feet are completely healed! I'm ready to go."

Together they stepped from the stream into the breathtaking beauty of the Garden of Eden.

CHAPTER SIX

There is something special about a garden. A true garden is planned by one who loves flowers, plants, and trees and arranges them in such a way that each plant and flower ties into the whole and yet, at the same time, has its own beauty enhanced. The meadow with its sprinkling of flowers was beautiful, but the Garden of Eden, planted and arranged by He who intimately knows the very nature of each plant and flower, was truly beyond description.

When Sally was home, she enjoyed working in the garden behind her house. Now, as she followed Gabby, her head first turned one way and then the other to catch the sights and sounds. She marveled at the exquisite setting of a clump of giant pansies, and the way a crimson climbing rose was entwined in the branches of an evergreen tree. She applauded the delicate shading of colors in the flowerbeds all around her. But these things were only a tiny part of the overall brilliant display of the Garden. There were arches of foliage setting one part of the Garden off from another. It was as if it had been divided into rooms with each room carrying its own glorious theme: spring, with vivid colors and delicate greens; summer, with gentle pastels; fall with a riot of yellows and browns; winter with more austere tones. All could be imagined in the displays she saw. And then there were fountains, streams, waterfalls, and water-lily covered ponds. And so much more! "Everything is simply beautiful," she exclaimed.

Sally was so busy looking around that she had fallen a distance behind Gabby. Bobby, following her, urged her to hurry and catch up. By this time Gabby had passed under an arch of roses into another area of the Garden. When they caught up, they found themselves in a large chamber-like room. To them, it appeared as if there were twinkling lights in the air which looked very much like giant dancing fireflies. Although the sun was high in the morning sky, the lights overshadowed it so much that it appeared dim compared to their brilliance. As they walked toward this brilliance, the lights erupted into a fireworks display of continually shifting, blending colors which seemed to rain down around them. "Welcome to The Garden of Eden," a deep voice said from the midst of the lights.

Later, Bobby would say the voice had such a richness and variety of tone that it was as if an entire orchestra were speaking.

"Welcome to the Garden. I am the Father of Lights, The Creator." At the sound of the voice, the lights danced. It seemed as if a thousand rainbows were dancing -- up, down, all around. "I change not. No man has ever seen Me. But, even though you cannot see My essence, you can still know Me by some of My names:

Yes, I am Lord; My name is mighty.

My name is everlasting,

My name upholds the universe,

And has from the very beginning.

I am Lord, My name is Holy,

And yet My name is Mercy,

Tender and Compassionate Friend;

In whom men can find victory.

My name is above every name.

At My name every knee shall bow down,

And every tongue shall confess,

I am worthy with glory to be crowned.

My name, My people shall forever bless.

I am Lord, My name is pure light,

A guide in the darkness of this world,

A strong tower, a cover in times of storm,

Protecting against the Serpent's darts at men hurled.

I am Lord, all My names spell love;

In My name men find their hope,

Protection in the hour of trouble,

So that with adversity they can cope.

Who can comprehend My name?

My name is opportunity,

Lending strength to achieve all that becomes a man.

Giving grace to grow in truth, in purity.

I am Lord, My name is an open door,

The gateway to true humanity --

And My name is ever so much more.

My name declares all My majesty."

As the voice spoke, the dancing lights changed into even more intricate patterns. At times they formed shapes: a great lion, a snow white lamb, and then, what appeared to be a dim figure on a cross. "I change not. Learn My names and you will come to know Me. I am present with you here and I am also present with Adam in the next glen. Come and see." As He said this, the lights gradually faded. After they were totally gone, His presence could still be felt lingering in the room. Even without the lights, everything in the room looked brighter and more alive.

While the voice was speaking, the children kept their heads bowed, feeling that it was a small gesture of honor and the proper thing to do. Seeing this, Gabby approved of their attitude of worship. "When I first saw you, I knew both of you were special and intelligent. Yes! Yes! I did! That's why I was willing to be your guide. But despite being intelligent and special, somehow, you still managed to get into trouble in this sin-free world."

The children didn't understand what he was talking about and looked at him quizzingly, so he continued, "Trouble! You know -- falling into the pond!" They were relieved that's all he was talking about; they were afraid they might have done something really bad. "Your presence here has been approved and confirmed -- you have received a special invitation from God, Himself. So, I guess I'll have to continue looking after you no matter what trouble you get into. Yes! Yes! I will!" One could detect satisfaction in his words as he added, "We still have to travel to the next glen to see Adam. Hurry! Hurry! We're late! Yes! We are!"

Beyond the chamber of lights, a long corridor of evergreens arched high overhead. After the light display, the corridor gave them the sensation of marching down the aisle of a great cathedral. In awe they walked in silence. Finally Bobby broke the silence, "What did the High Lord mean when He told us to know His names? I thought I saw the lights form the shape of a lion and a lamb. Is His name Lion or Lamb?"

"He gave us only a few of His names and hinted at others. And yes! Yes! Lion is one of them -- He's called The Lion of the Tribe of Judah. He's also called The Lamb -- The Lamb that takes away the sins of the world. But you'll understand more after you've seen what sin does to the world. Yes! Yes!"

When two large black and white rabbits hopped past them, Bobby realized they were the first animals they had seen in the Garden. "Gabby, why haven't we seen any large animals? We've only seen birds, bees and a few butterflies. And of course, Chippy-Chip."

"The animals are all at a meeting. We should be there, too. Yes! Yes! We should!" Chuckling, he added, "And, if you don't stop asking so many questions, we'll be later than we already are."

"What's so funny?" Sally questioned. "Why are you laughing? Was it something Bobby said?"

"No! Oh dear! No! I wasn't laughing at what Bobby said; I was laughing at what the rabbits were saying as they hopped by."

"But I didn't hear them say anything!" Sally said.

"Oh! Dear!" He sighed, "I'm going to have to try to explain again. Yes! I am! And I'm so terrible at explanations. Aren't there many different languages in your world? If you don't understand them, they all sound strange. No! No! That's not a good way to explain . . . Different languages have different sounds. Right! There, that's better! Yes! Yes! Different sounds. Yes! Some languages have whistles and, in others, the speaker's tongue has to click to form sounds. Rabbits speak a language that doesn't have any sounds. Only when they're in distress and need help, can they call out in an audible voice. Oh! Dear me! I'm trying to be as clear as I can, but I can't expect you'll understand. Oh! No! No!"

But Bobby did understand. "You mean rabbits use sign language like a deaf person?"

"Yes! Yes! Of course! That's exactly what I'm saying. Rabbits use their ears, noses and lips to speak but don't make sounds with their mouths."

"Is that why rabbits twitch their noses?"

"Of course, Bobby! Yes! Rabbits can talk rapidly with their sign language. One of the quickest ways is for them to twitch their noses."

Sally repeated her earlier question. "But Gabby, what were they saying?"

"Yes! Yes! Of course! What did they say? Well, Mr. Rabbit was complaining about his wife stopping at each pool of water to use the reflection in the water as a mirror. Not only that but she also made him stop at least ten times while she brushed her whiskers -- she wanted them to look just right. Mr. Rabbit wasn't too happy about stopping because he felt her whiskers looked fine -- in fact, he thought they were quite beautiful and didn't need brushing!"

"What's so funny about that?" she asked.

"Oh! He was afraid that the tortoises might beat them to the meeting. Yes! Afraid!"

They reached the end of the evergreen corridor and found themselves in the largest open space they had seen so far. The ground was carpeted with velvety green grass, so soft that, as they walked, their huge heavy feet made no sound. Far ahead, they saw the dim outline of two trees. Radiating toward the trees, like spokes on a wheel, were hedges -- hedges trimmed in animal shapes. The hedge nearest to them was trimmed to resemble rabbits. Rabbits playing, rabbits eating, rabbits sleeping -- rabbits in every possible pose. The hedge on their left showed a gallery of cats. Sally, who loved cats, wanted to stop and study them. They had to persuade her to keep moving. Further away, Bobby saw hedges shaped like dinosaurs. He wished he were closer so he could see them better.

As they drew closer to the trees, the same lights they had seen earlier were shimmering in the sky. They knew they were almost to the place of the meeting.

"We're approaching the very center of the Garden. Yes! Yes! The very center. The tree on your right is the Tree of of Life and and the one on the left is the Tree of Knowledge of Good and Evil. The meeting will take place just beyond the trees. Walking under the Tree of Life is the shortest way for us to get there. Yes! Yes! It is!"

Sally's voice sounded hesitant. "Gabby, what's the Tree of Life?"

"The Tree of Life grows wherever God makes His home. It has twelve different kinds of fruit -- one for each month of the year. The fruit can remove sadness and sorrow from the heart and, depending on the season of the year, bring joy, courage, hope, peace, and unselfish love. Yes! Yes! It can! The fruit from the Tree of Life has the same golden color as the fruit on the Tree of Knowledge of Good and Evil. If anyone eats the fruit from the Tree of Life, they will never die.

But, for you, the fruit from both trees is forbidden. Yes! Absolutely forbidden! You are guests here and it wouldn't be right for you to eat the fruit. No! It wouldn't! If you did eat it, never again could you return to your own time because you would no longer be satisfied there. No! You wouldn't! But, don't worry, God won't let that happen. If you try to eat any of the fruit, He will immediately transport you back to your own world."

As they came closer, they saw that the Tree of Life was loaded with golden, grapefruit-sized fruit shimmering in the sunshine.

Looking at the Tree of Knowledge of Good and Evil, they observed that, just as Gabby had told them, its fruit shone as if it had been carved from pure gold.

CHAPTER SEVEN

Passing under the branches of the Tree of Life, Gabby and the children found that the grassy field just beyond was a natural amphitheater filled with large and small animals. By approaching the way they had, they found they were in the very front of the amphitheater. To their right were the dancing lights, but they were more subdued in brightness than earlier, hardly more than a faint shimmering in the air. They were dim because today it was Adam, the caretaker and newly formed king of this world, who would hold center stage, not The Creator. The children's eyes were drawn to Adam who was standing straight and majestic between them and the dancing lights. In the children's world he definitely would have been considered a giant. He was over seven feet tall and had muscles like a professional athlete in his prime. Bobby tried to imprint an impression of Adam's face in his mind. *Noble, strong, righteous* -- these were some of the terms which he thought of to describe Adam's appearance. *Truly suited to be a king,* was the phrase that entered and stayed in his mind.

They continued to gaze at Adam. His skin was as bronze as if he had spent weeks in the sun; he had short, curly black hair. His face, neck, arms, and legs were the only parts they could see since the trunk of his body was encased in light and hidden from them. A strong light arose from his presence and made his body shine so brightly that it couldn't be seen.

Sally had always liked to dream about the kings and queens she read about in her history books. Once she had even seen the President of the United States in person. Of course, she had also seen him many times on television. The difference between Adam, The President, and the kings and queens of old was similar to comparing a black and white photograph to a color photograph. No! Rather like comparing a photograph to real life. Adam possessed a whole different dimension of glory than she had ever seen in a person. She wondered if perhaps her eyes hadn't adjusted to the bright colors of the new world. Or... maybe looking at the bright light shining from Adam had partially blinded her.

The children were mesmerized and couldn't take their eyes away from Adam's commanding appearance. Suddenly, they again heard the rich, full voice of The Creator saying to the animals, "Come! Come to Adam!" Out of the ranks of the animals, two young bears came forward and began speaking to Adam in woofs and grunts.

Gabby and the children had stopped a short distance from the animals to observe what was happening. They remained close but didn't join them. This was a perfect spot to see and hear everything that was happening. Gabby turned to the children and said, "Pay attention, for now you will see some of the truth you are here to see. Yes! Yes! Adam is as men were meant to be, made in the image of God, made to show His character on earth. Watch and learn; watch and listen because there is much more for you to see and know. Yes! Yes! There is!"

The children's attention swung back to Adam in time to hear him say. "I name you Mr. and Mrs. Bear -- loyal, courageous protectors of the Garden, lovers of berries and all things sweet. You will be valuable helpers by protecting the Garden and helping to enlarge its borders." After hearing this, the bears turned and ambled back to rejoin the other animals. Bobby searched the animal crowd and was amused to see that, yes, the tortoises were indeed ahead of the rabbits in the lineup of animals pressing forward to meet King Adam.

Bobby's musings were interrupted by the voice of The Creator saying, "Come!"

Two more animals left the group and rushed up to Adam. "Who are you?" he asked them.

"We're master engineers -- at your service," they chittered. "We're the tireless builders of dams and the makers of ponds."

"I name you... Mr. and Mrs. Beaver. You will be in charge of all water works in the Garden. You will see they are kept clean and that the streams don't overflow their banks. You will also be in charge of building new ponds and -- when we extend the Garden -- all irrigation to the new areas. I'm pleased to have you as my new helpers."

As the beavers scampered back to join the other animals, Sally, who had been watching intently, commented, "None of these animals appear to be fierce. Even the bears look gentle, like cuddly teddy bears. And I don't see any wolves. Where are they? Gabby, didn't you tell us they were the helpers of the Evil One?"

"They aren't yet; but, when Adam is no longer king of the animals, they will come. Yes! Yes! They will! What you now see is how the animal world was meant to be. The entire animal world is vegetarian. All animals eat fruits, roots, and plants -- none eat meat. And none of the men who follow The Creator will eat meat either, that is, until much later in history. It isn't until after the world is nearly destroyed by flood that men begin to eat meat. Perhaps someday you'll be allowed to see the truth of the flood. Most people from your world and time don't believe in the flood any more than they believe in the truth of creation. No! They don't! Sally, only after evil from the Evil One changes the nature of some of the animals, will you see the wolves. Yes! The animals you see here today are the ancestors of all the animals in your time. Yes! They are! All dogs, wolves, coyotes, and foxes come from the one pair of dogs now standing before Adam."

After hearing Adam give the dogs his blessing and naming them Mr. and Mrs. Dog, Sally said, "I'm confused! Why is Adam giving the animals names they already have?"

"It is a little confusing, isn't it? Oh! Dear! Am I going to have to explain again? He's giving them names because, at this time, they don't have names yet. He's trying to give them names that fit them. No! No! That doesn't help much, does it? Let me try again. Yes! Adam is naming the animals because it's the beginning, but you recognize the names that he's giving them because you're not from the beginning; you're from the future. Oh! Dear me! Sometimes I even confuse myself. Yes! Yes! I do!"

"It's like traveling back in time and hearing your mom give you your name," Bobby commented. "That would be really wild!"

"I think it would be fun to hear my mother choose my name," Sally broke in. "If I were there to help, my name would either be Marcy, Jessica, or Alice. I think those names are much prettier than Sally." At the idea, she clapped her front feet together with joy.

Bobby changed the subject. "I think it's marvelous that every animal in our world came from these. I can name most of the wild animals that are cousins to domestic animals. All these animals before us, whether wild or tame, have the same parents. Not just wolves and dogs, but also cattle, ducks, chickens, turkeys, pigs and sheep. What have I forgotten? Oh! Yes! The horses! But some animals, like the bears, have never been tame. They've always been wild. The only place you'll see a tame bear is at the circus and even they are not completely tame. Gabby, have all the animals not living with man been touched by the Evil One?"

"In one sense the whole world is to be touched by the Evil One. But more about that later. And no! Oh! No! The wild animals haven't been touched by evil any more than domestic animals. At least not all of them. Haven't you heard of pet dogs that become vicious and turn against their master? Dogs are meant to be man's best friend and yet they can be dangerous. An evil owner can cause a good dog to become surly and mean. Yes! Yes! They can! And then you hear stories of a wild member of the cat family being tamed and becoming a good pet to -- "

Sally interrupted. "I don't believe any cat can truly be tamed. They like comfort and may curl up in your lap and purr, but they still remain independent and aloof. Most of the time they wander around doing their own thing as if living a secret life." Then changing the subject, she said, "Gabby, are you claiming that every tame and wild rabbit in our world came from the two we just saw -- the giant hares, cottontails, and jackrabbits? Rabbits come in so many different kinds and colors, and have such different coats -- some soft and others bristly." Sally knew a lot about rabbits because of a paper she had written about them in school.

"Yes! Indeed! Yes! I said *all*. But, shush! Pay attention! Listen to what Adam's saying to the dinosaurs!"

Two large dinosaurs were standing before Adam, speaking to him in hissing tones. Their heavily scaled bodies, long slender necks, and heads that appeared to be too large for their bodies, made them resemble giant lizards. The children couldn't understand their hissing speech. Then Adam spoke, "Mr. and Mrs. Dragon of the fiery breath, I proclaim you to be Guardians of the Garden and official openers of the custard acorn fruit."

"He called them dragons!" Bobby excitedly exclaimed. "I thought they were just large lizards. I didn't believe dragons existed -- only in fairy tales! I don't see any wings. Gabby, can they fly?"

"These can't, but there are smaller bird-like dinosaurs that can. Yes! Dragons do exist and can squirt a boiling hot, fiery vapor from their nostrils. Yes! They can! This ability isn't unusual! No! No! It isn't! Did you know that in your world there are insects called bombadier beetles that also squirt a fiery liquid at an enemy? Here in the Garden, dragons use their hot breath to open the custard acorn fruit. Nothing tastes quite as good as a custard acorn. Oh! Dear me! No! I do hope you get to try some. Yes! I do!"

"I sure wouldn't want to fight with a dragon after it becomes evil," Bobby commented. "They're frightening enough to look at, even when they're not breathing fire."

A steady stream of animals, two by two, male and female, continued approaching Adam all morning and into late afternoon. Each received a name and a blessing from Adam, the one appointed by God to be caretaker of the Garden. As they listened, the children learned about the character, loyalty, courage, and strength of the various animals. They also learned more about flexibility, hospitality, generosity and many other wonderful things. Sally said, "God sure gave Adam a lot of responsibility -- he has to take care of all the animals."

"You're right! Yes! Yes! You are! It is a lot of responsibility. But don't you think it also gives him a great deal of satisfaction?"

"He has to work harder than the animals!" Bobby exclaimed. "In our world the king is served by his subjects. Here, it's reversed -- Adam, the ruler, serves the subjects."

"That's right! Yes! Yes! Adam displays greatness by serving others."

Finally the long line of animals came to an end, and they scattered to their assigned homes inside and outside of the Garden. After watching them leave, Gabby and the children listened as Adam spoke to the Shimmering Lights. "Father of Lights, I didn't find a companion, a helpmate, for me."

"You didn't find one as there wasn't one suited to be your companion. You saw that I gave each animal a companion. Male and female I created them. And, as you spoke to them, you saw the joy and pride in the intimacy of their relationships. For you, I have something better. Trust in Me!"

CHAPTER EIGHT

As Gabby and the children watched, the lights, which had remained dim throughout the naming of the animals, gradually grew brighter until those watching were almost blinded by the brilliance. Once again the sun seemed dim in comparison. The children realized it wasn't an illusion -- the sun actually was growing dimmer -- as if its light were being eclipsed. Even the sky was changing, taking on the colors of evening though the sun was high in the sky and sunset was hours away. As the false twilight deepened, the lights appeared to shine even more brightly and entered into a majestic dance, with movements in time with the enchanting celestial music. It was impossible to describe the sights and sounds which swelled up in the empty amphitheater.

A sudden overwhelming tiredness came over Bobby and he fought to keep his eyes open. Soon, he realized he was fighting a losing battle. He looked over at Sally and saw that she, also, was nodding. He was too comfortable to move even a single muscle. Finally his eyes closed and he drifted into deep, dark, and dreamless sleep.

It seemed like only a moment had passed when his eyes popped open. However, he realized he must have slept for more than an hour because the sun was slowly setting behind the western hills. He could still hear the celestial music -- muted -- but clear. He was at peace. Everything felt right and proper, just as it should.

The lights were still dancing, but again their brilliance was nothing more than a shimmering. As Bobby looked at the lights, he noticed Adam was lying on the ground asleep. *So Adam was also caught in the sleeping spell,* Bobby thought. Then he noticed someone was lying beside Adam. As he watched, this figure rose to her feet. He knew this had to be Eve! She was tall, graceful and had light blond hair which tumbled in cascades down to her waist. Her eyes were dark blue and, like Adam, she was clothed in light. But, the light that wrapped around her was different -- it gradually changed color. These color changes fascinated Bobby. At first her light was pure white, then gradually changed to soft purple, and finally to deep blue. Then the blue disappeared and was replaced by brilliant emerald.

"Welcome Eve! Welcome to the Garden!" The voice from the dancing lights was saying.

"What shall I wear for my lord at his awakening?" Eve asked. Her voice was soft, musical and filled with laughter. As she spoke, the light surrounding her changed to a flaming red.

Hearing her, Adam stretched and rose to his feet. In awe, he silently gazed at her, then whispered, "You are woman for you have been taken out of man. Flesh of my flesh and bone of my bone. You shall be dearer to me than my very breath. You shall be called Eve, the mother of all living, the mother of all men."

"Where did she come from?" Sally demanded of Gabby. She had awakened shortly after Bobby and was totally engrossed by the scene in front of her.

"While you were sleeping, The Creator fashioned Eve from one of Adam's ribs. Yes! He did!"

"Adam looks the same as he did before; he's no smaller," Bobby remarked.

"And Eve is almost as tall as he is," Sally added. "She's absolutely beautiful. How could she possibly be one of his ribs?"

"The Creator fashioned this whole world from nothing. You've already seen the wonders of His creative ability. Yes! Yes! You have! And remember, God never takes something without leaving more behind than what there was to begin with. When God asks you to give something up, don't forget what I have told you. Oh! No! Don't forget! God's Son, Jesus, proved this to be true when He took a small boy's lunch of five loaves and two small fish and fed over five thousand men, women, and children. Why, when they were done, they still had twelve large baskets of food left! But that's another story. Another time! Yes! Yes! It is! Adam isn't any less now that Eve is here -- he's as much Adam as he ever was. God didn't want man to be alone. Adam, by himself, wasn't complete, but with Eve he is. Remember these truths when you return to your world."

"They're absolutely perfect for one another," Sally said dreamily. Like most girls her age, she enjoyed daydreaming about romance.

"What you see here in the Garden is perfection. Yes! Yes! 'For this cause a man shall leave his father and his mother, and shall cleave to his wife, and they shall become one flesh.' That's what it says in The Creator's Book. Adam and Eve are different from one another, and yet they are truly one because they have been united by God in heart and purpose."

"Gabby, I don't understand. How can they be different and still be one?" Bobby asked.

"Oh! Dear me! I do hate explaining! Yes! I do! I always get so mixed up! If I told you that day is different from night, would you believe me? I'm sure you learned in school that day and night are created by one complete turn of the earth. Both day and night belong to a bigger whole. As the earth turns on its axis, one-half is always in darkness and the other half is in daylight. Oh! Dear! What is it I'm trying to say? You wouldn't know what day is if you didn't have night, and you wouldn't know what night is without having day. God said, '*And the morning and the evening were the first day.*' Do you understand that it takes both day and night together to make up one day?"

"I understand how one car is made of many different parts, but I don't understand how two people can be one," Bobby admitted.

"Jim and Jerry, the twins at school, seem like one," Sally said. "I used to get them mixed up all the time."

"You're getting closer to understanding. Yes! Yes! You are! You probably have difficulty telling them apart because they look alike. Tell me Bobby, how do you tell them apart?"

"That's easy! Jim likes football and usually has grass stains on his clothes. Jerry, his brother, enjoys music -- especially playing his trumpet. He's fussy about his looks and his clothes are always neat and clean."

"So you tell them apart, not only by their outward appearances, but also by inside differences -- by what their interests are. In true oneness the outward appearance may be different but things on the inside are the same. On the inside, Adam and Eve are twins -- they're alike. A person's outward appearance isn't that important. No! It isn't! Adam and Eve's goals and desires are so identical that, if you ask a question, you'll get the same answer from each of them. True oneness will always be found on the inside. Yes! It will!"

"In our world, when a couple gets married, they expect to live happily ever after. At least that's the way most romance stories end. But, I have a lot of friends whose parents are divorced," Sally said soberly.

"There's still a memory in your world of how marriage was meant to be! Yes! Yes! There is! And that memory draws people to marriage. But, what they don't realize is that there can be no true unity in marriage as long as they focus only on their own selfish desires and not the desires of their mate. People need to learn to seek likeness on the inside rather than wasting time looking for harmony on the outside. Yes! Very important! Marriage will never be perfect but it can be very good. It's as close as people can come in experiencing that two can be one. Yes! It is! But, of course, before you will fully understand what I'm telling you, you'll have to grow up. Learning to look on the inside will help when the time comes for you to choose a person to marry."

"Gabby, how can you find someone who's like you on the inside?" Sally asked. "Some of my friends' parents do things together such as playing tennis, but it doesn't seem to help much. Tricia tells me her parents fight so much she wishes she could come and live with me."

Gabby answered her question with a question. "Sally, who prepared Eve for Adam?"

"The Creator. The Father of Lights."

"Right! And it's the same in your world. He's the One who can guide you! Learn to listen to Him! He's the only One who knows what's on the inside -- in the hearts of men. He must be a partner in a relationship if it is to be right on the inside! Yes! Yes! He must!"

"Why did The Creator make Eve out of Adam's rib?" Bobby asked.

"I know why!" Sally piped up. "To show they're one!"

"Sally, I know that. But it seems there should be more to it. That's why I asked Gabby."

"Although you've seen these events as they happened, your world is so different that it's difficult for you to understand. Oh! Dear me! How do I explain? I know! Bobby, tell me, how did it feel when you fell into the pool of water?"

"My feet hurt and, for a while, I felt sick."

"True! But that's not the answer I was looking for. Not sickness but health! Yes! That's it! Your feet healed quickly. Health is the answer. There is a wholeness here that gives one a sense that all parts of the body belong together. Yes! There is! For example, if you should accidentally cut off a finger or a toe, you will strongly feel its loss. However, if you pick up the severed part and place it back where it belongs, it will quickly reunite with the body. That's how Adam is; he feels the absence of his rib -- that something is missing. And, of course, the part that is missing is now Eve. This is the oneness that God has given them, a unity that each strongly feels."

"I think I'm beginning to see why The Creator made Eve the way He did," Bobby said. "Somehow it wouldn't be right for Adam to feel that Eve was made from a part of his foot."

"I agree," Sally said. "Even if God had used a part of Adam's head, it still wouldn't have been right. Imagine feeling that you were empty headed -- that a part of your head was missing. Though, I suppose, it might be good if it were an ear so people might listen to one another. Sometimes it seems as if my dad never listens to me."

"Only by making Eve from Adam's side could God The Creator give them true oneness. It's good you've witnessed this. Yes! Yes! It is! But there is another reason God created Eve the way He did. Yes! There is! Can you guess what it might be?" Gabby waited for an answer from the children. Seeing them shake their heads, he continued, "Adam gave up part of his body so Eve could be formed. God was showing Adam that it always takes sacrifice to gain true oneness, true unity. Yes! Yes! It does!"

During their discussion, night had fallen and they could see a multitude of bright stars overhead. The dancing lights had left, and the Garden lay in the stillness of night. Although it was dark, Adam and Eve's pure, noble, majestic faces could be clearly seen from the glow that surrounded them. Eve's light was pure white with a deep blue fringe along the edge that exactly matched her eyes.

"Come!" Gabby said. "We must go to the place in the Garden that has been made ready for us. Tomorrow will soon be here and it, too, has important lessons."

CHAPTER NINE

That night Bobby dreamed he was home sitting in front of the living room fireplace, talking with his mom and dad about the planets. In his dream he was telling them the planets were very young, not old as he had been taught in school. As he awoke, it felt as if he were leaving reality and entering into a dream. He heard music -- music as deep and resonant as thunder. And yet, at the same time, it was as soft as the caress of a warm summer breeze! He opened his eyes and found he was lying in what appeared to be a large green room.

As his eyes focused, he realized he was in a *living room* -- not a room to live in, but a room formed by *living things*. He was lying on a carpet of grass so thick and soft it felt as if he were resting on a soft, fluffy, sheepskin. The walls were hedges but unlike any hedges he had ever seen. Each had a pattern similar to a mural painted on a wall. The patterns consisted of a background of dark green leaves, woven together with paler green leaves and other leaves laced with white. Overhead the sky was blocked from view by a thick network of vines covered by leaves that were almost white but with just a hint of green. As he listened, he heard a faint rustling sound that wasn't part of the music but harmonized with it. He realized the rustling noise was coming from the vines overhead. As he watched, the mat of vines began to unravel. They were untangling themselves, waving in time to the music, shaking their leaves as they unwound. A hole appeared in the vines, allowing the early morning sun to send a beam of sunlight onto the soft grass where Gabby and Sally were sleeping. Rapidly, the hole increased in size. As the vines untangled, they wove themselves into the familiar hedge walls of the Garden. Soon the leaf and vine ceiling had vanished and the sun was upon them with all its brilliance.

The music became louder and Bobby heard someone singing. He recognized the voice; it was The Creator, Himself, who was singing. "Behold everything I have created! Look and see! Look and enjoy! For all My creation is very good!"

The words, though not loud, had an intensity that demanded attention. They penetrated a person's innermost being, filling both heart and mind.

"Rejoice, oh creation; rejoice with Me!

Rejoice in Me ye fish of the sea

You live in waters of unsurpassed beauty.

Rejoice oh ye birds flying on high

To you I have given the delights of the sky.

Rejoice oh ye beasts of the field

To you the earth her fruit abundantly will yield.

Rejoice greatly, Adam, father of man

Dominion over all earth is placed in your hand.

Rejoice, rejoice all that draw breath

Today is the seventh day, day given for rest.

Rejoice, rejoice for I all life truly bless."

Suddenly, from every direction, Bobby heard other voices lifted in song with The Creator to form a grand, joyful chorus. He heard birds whistling and chirping, the yapping of dogs, horses neighing, and many other animal voices. Some he could recognize; others he could not. Then, near to where he was standing, he heard Adam and Eve join in. "We rejoice, we rejoice that You are our Lord. We rejoice, we rejoice; we will follow Your Word. We rejoice, we rejoice, in all you have done. We rejoice, we rejoice, in our life just begun."

Their voices blended with the others in a glorious hymn of praise.

"I wish I could understand what they're singing. It sounds so wonderful and beautiful!" Sally said.

"Soon you will understand the language of every voice you hear! Yes! Yes! You will! Today is supposed to be a day of rest for those in the Garden but we have work to do. Yes! Not hard work, but still work. I need to help get your ears tuned into the languages of this world. Not that you're not doing well! Oh! No! You've been real troupers! Not a whimper or complaint! But you will learn more when you understand everything that's being said. There are many, many languages. Some have only a few words, while others have many. Every animal has its own language. Yes! They do! We shall be very, very busy. Yes! But first let's eat a good breakfast; we need strength for this day." Gabby stood and walked to the entrance of the room.

Just outside the entrance, there was a stack of fruit. Reaching down, Gabby picked some up, and handed a piece to each of them. Bobby couldn't tell what kind of fruit it was by its appearance or taste, but it sure was good. He ate and ate until he was full. "Gabby, where did this fruit come from? Did you pick it while we were sleeping?"

"No! Oh! No! I didn't pick it! On the day of rest, The Creator supplies all our needs. He knows exactly what they are and satisfies them all. Yes! He gives us just enough -- not too little or too much. Yes! Just enough! That's one of the things he does to teach us trust."

"If this is a day of rest, isn't it wrong for us to work?"

"If it were wrong, Bobby, I wouldn't suggest it. Oh! Dear me! No! I wouldn't! The Creator made the day of rest so man could more fully enjoy life. The greatest joy a man can have is getting to know his Creator better. That's why it's proper for everyone to rejoice in Him on the day of rest. Yes! It is! The only true rest a man can have is when he's resting in God and relying on His provision. Yes! It is! You're already enjoying the day so perhaps you have a glimpse of what I'm trying to say. There are still things you need to learn and understand in order to more fully enjoy the Garden and to better grasp the truth. Yes! There are! So on the day of rest, it is proper to learn things that help you to understand."

Sally, who had been listening quietly, questioned him. "Gabby, if the animals are only one day old, I don't understand. How can they know so much?"

"You don't have to fully understand. No! You don't! All you need to know and believe is that God gave them their knowledge. Every animal already knows everything it needs so that it can do what The Creator intended. Yes! Yes! They do! Some of that knowledge will be passed down to their children as instincts that come straight from The Father. And just as you learn from your parents, the animals also will have to teach their children. Yes!"

Bobby had to know more. "Do animals have memories? Memories of things from before -- when there wasn't a before -- or are their memories only one day old?"

"They have thoughts that seem like memories to them. Yes! Yes! They know how to do things they've never done before. Oh! Dear me! It's so confusing! Yes! It is! But I don't know how to say it any other way."

Remembering his dream, Bobby asked, "Are their memories like dreams?"

"That's as good a way of saying it as any. Yes! Yes! It is! What Adam, Eve and the animals remember is similar to a dream. Yes!

Now they're starting to live out their memories in a real way. It's very simple and, at the same time, very difficult. Yes! Oh my! Yes! I do wish I could explain better! Indeed I do! But now we have to start working on animal speech fundamentals so you'll be ready for tomorrow."

Sally teased her friend. "Bobby, I'm surprised at you! You're asking Gabby more questions than I am, and I'm supposed to be the talkative one. You never talk this much at school!"

The next hour went by quickly as Gabby taught them how to shape their lips and hold their tongues to make a variety of sounds such as squeals, barks, clicks, and even buzzing. Sally was a quick learner and told Bobby how to shape his lips to make a squeal.

He made a face at her. "Maybe I can't squeal very well but I can growl better than you."

"No you can't!"

Her reply started a fun time of growling, barking, squealing and making faces at one another.

Gabby interrupted their fun saying, "Enough! Enough! Practice listening! You need to sharpen your hearing skills so you can tell the difference between one sound and another sound that is similar. Yes! Yes! You do!"

"How come we've been working so hard and aren't tired?" Bobby asked after several hours.

Gabby laughed. "Because you're in the Land of the Beginning. Here, knowledge is a gift from God that doesn't have to be learned by hard work and study. No! No! It doesn't! What you're learning is similar to pulling out an instinct The Creator has placed in your mind. Yes! Yes! It is! Knowledge flows into you just like water into a sponge. It's already in your mind; you just have to take it out. Back home you have to put it in before you can take it out."

"Wouldn't it be great if I could learn my lessons at school this easily," Sally commented. "Gabby, when we return home, will we remember all this so it will help us in school?"

"Even if you did remember the languages, they wouldn't be much help to you, because, except in a very limited way, the animals in your world have lost their ability to speak. No! Oh my! No! You won't remember! But I wouldn't be surprised to find you're very good in human languages. Yes! You'll retain the ability to duplicate difficult sounds which will make it possible for you to easily learn languages. Remember though, you'll have to work harder than you do here. Yes! Much harder!"

Bobby hungered for more truths. "Gabby, why do some scientists say that animals are evolving -- getting smarter, bigger and better? The languages of the animals in the Garden clearly show they're much smarter than the ones back home. And obviously they're bigger and healthier, too.

"Yes! Yes! Of course they're bigger, healthier, and smarter here than in your time. But don't forget, even here, there's still big differences between the different types of animals. Yes! Yes! Big differences! Some, as you know, have a limited language while others can say almost anything. But no animal compares to man. No! They don't! Only man is made in the image of God. Yes! Only man! Yes! Animals see things only as they are, not as they can be. They can't understand concepts like beauty or duty and most would rather play than work. They recognize whether they're hungry or full and happy or sad -- but not much more. That's why they need man to watch out for them. Yes! They do! The animals' limitatations aren't true of God's messengers, the angels, who come from another realm. it's a mystery but for a time these messengers are even higher than man. Sometimes at God's bidding, they may visit this world. Yes! Yes! At other times, they may take the form of a lower creature but still retain knowledge and wisdom greater than man's. Yes! But I haven't answered your question. No! No! I haven't! It's just that men don't always want the truth. They want to believe they can make the world bigger and better without The Creator. Yes! They do! So they pretend it's their effort that causes things to get bigger and better. They are pretending -- lying -- even to themselves! Yes! They are!"

"Do they believe their own lies?"

"Some do, Bobby! Yes! Yes! They do!"

"They must," agreed Sally. "Otherwise, why do scientists tell us all animals started from nothing but chemical soup? Do they really believe, like my science teacher, that after a million years the descendents of a tadpole can become a whale?"

"They say these things because they forget that God, The Creator, made everything. Yes! They do! You've seen the world here in the Land of the Beginning as it truly is, including the animals living peacefully together. Yes! Yes! You have! What you read in science books are only guesses by people who don't really know. Their guesses show the world as they would like it, not as it really is. They're trying to make a world in which men rule over everything and have no responsibility to The Creator. But enough for now; you'll understand more later. Yes! Yes! Let's return to our lessons."

They worked until late in the evening to learn languages they couldn't understand the day before. They studied the rabbit's sign language, the cat's meow, the dog's bark, and many others. The sound made by the whistling swans gave Bobby the most trouble. As a boy he was a good whistler; however, as a Tyrannosaurus, he had a hard time puckering up to blow air through his lips.

"That's okay! Yes! Yes! It is! Even if you can't speak their language, you'll still understand what the swans are saying."

Sally enjoyed talking like a laughing hyena. Every time she spoke their language she ended up laughing so hard that she forgot what it was she was trying to say. "The Creator must surely have a sense of humor to invent a language like this one."

"He sure does," Gabby responded. "He's author of all! Yes! He is!"

They worked steadily, only stopping now and then for a snack. When they finally quit, it was well after dark. "Now you have a thousand tongues with which to praise God! Yes! Yes! You do!"

"A thousand!" Bobby repeated. "We didn't learn that many."

"It probably seems like you did. Yes! Yes!" Gabby laughed.

There was one piece of fruit left for each of them for a bedtime snack. It was exactly enough. As they lay down to sleep, they were completely satisfied.

CHAPTER TEN

When Bobby and Sally awoke the next morning in the room surrounded by hedges with the roof of vines overhead, memories of the exciting events of the previous days came rushing back. As they watched, the vines unraveled and soon the sun was shining down on them. The night before, when they first entered this room, Gabby had announced, "This is it! Yes! It is! We're here!" Yesterday, they had been so busy studying that they never left the room or even thought to ask what it was like outside. All they knew about the place was that it was *here*, wherever *here* was.

"Gabby, what is this place? I mean, where are we?" Sally asked.

"This is part of the inner Garden where Adam and Eve work. Most of the Garden is planned from here. Yes! Yes! It is! You might say this is their headquarters. As keepers of the knowledge of the Garden, all Tyrannosauruses are assigned rooms close to Adam and Eve. Last night, after hearing them sing so near, you should have guessed they were close. Yes! Yes!"

"I'm hungry! I looked outside and there isn't any fruit. What are we going to do if we don't find something to eat -- sit around and look at hedges all day?" Bobby asked.

"Why don't you go see, rather than just sitting there? But, before you do, I have something to tell you. Yes! Yes! I do! Today, I won't be your guide. No! No! I won't! Bobby, you'll be going with Adam, and Sally will be with Eve. Oh! Dear me! What else was I supposed to tell you? Oh! Yes! That's it! You aren't allowed to say anything about the future or your world. That would never do! Dear me! No! You can only talk about things that presently exist in the Garden."

Hearing who they would be with, the children excitedly rushed through the gate in the hedges and found themselves in a small garden within the Garden. A stream bubbled past their feet as it wound its way through the Garden. On the other side of the stream were patches of vegetables they recognized -- carrots, peas, corn, cabbage, tomatoes and others. And there were many which were totally unfamiliar -- some with smooth green skin and pink dots -- some covered with pale green fuzz and yellow stripes. Looking at them, Bobby decided he wasn't about to eat anything that looked that strange. He knew everything he had eaten in the Garden so far had been delicious, but decided he wasn't going to take a chance with these vegetables. Some plants resembled cactus, and others appeared to be thornless thistles. Ferns were growing near the stream, and the area was dotted with a variety of mushrooms. Near the vegetables were different kinds of dwarf fruit trees -- peach, apricot, pear, lemon, lime, apple, orange and others.

They quickly crossed the shallow stream and soon were busy eating. Bobby, who loved vegetables, first tried the tomatoes and then the mushrooms which he declared to be delicious. He was careful not to eat anything he didn't recognize. For dessert he decided to have an apple. Sally had bypassed the vegetables and gone directly to the fruit. First she ate a pear; then an orange, two apricots, and a plum. Discovering a large patch of raspberries under the apricot trees, she was now eating them for dessert. The fruit in the Garden was bigger and more nutritious than fruit back home. One plum alone weighed almost a pound. Though it didn't seem like they ate much, when they finished, they felt stuffed.

"Welcome to my pantry, keepers of the knowledge of the Garden. You must be Bobby Tyrannosaurus and you have to be Sally Tyrannosaurus." Eve had quietly come up behind them while they were eating. Continuing to speak in a low musical voice she said, "Sally, today you will be my companion! Bobby, you will be companion to Adam. He's expecting you. Go through the gate and you'll find him just past the peach trees." As Eve spoke, the children noticed the light she was wrapped in had a checkered effect of red and white patches. Just before rushing to join Adam, Bobby wondered if she had intentionally chosen them as her working colors.

"Sally, come with me. Come see my kitchen," she said leading Sally through an opening in the hedge to another area. This area was smaller than Eve's pantry but still as large as a basketball court. There was a small stream which meandered beside the hedge on the far side of the room. She noticed steam rising from the area where the stream disappeared under the hedge. Eve walked toward the rising steam with Sally following at her heels. When they got closer, Sally saw the steam wasn't coming from the stream but from six small pools of water bubbling up from the ground.

"Here is where I do my cooking. I don't have many recipies though," Eve said, reaching over and taking down a book hanging from a hedge near the pools.

Peeking over Eve's shoulder, Sally saw the words, *Garden Recipies* on the cover. As Eve opened it, Sally noticed only the first two pages had writing on them -- the rest were blank.

"Let's see. This morning I think I'll make stew. Chippy-Chip, would you please bring me two large chestnuts and about a dozen acorns?" At the sound of her voice, Chippy-Chip darted from beneath one of the hedges and peered up at her. He chittered and chattered and then scampered away to look for the nuts Eve had requested. Turning to one of the black and white rabbits watching from the corner, she continued, "Hoppy, will you please go to the pantry and bring me some vegetables for stew?" Hoppy listened intently to her instructions and then hopped through an opening in the hedge which led to the pantry.

"Sally, now it's your turn. Please hand me the pot that's on the shelf next to you."

The hedge beside Sally had been trimmed flat on top so that it resembled a table. From a shelf cut into it, she spotted a golden gleam. Reaching in, she pulled out a large golden pot. "That pot is made from gold that comes from Havilah," Eve said. "Gold from there is very good!"

Sally, who was in awe of Eve and hadn't spoken since seeing her, finally found the courage to say something. "Isn't all gold good?"

"Yes, but because gold from Havilah is found in such large nuggets, it's easy to make into pots and other things. That's why it's so good. And, of course, the pot made from it, is also good. One can store food cooked in a gold pot and its flavor won't change. However, food cooked and stored in an earthen pot takes on an earthen flavor, and food stored in a gourd quickly becomes flat and stale. As you see, I have all three kinds -- but my gold pot is the best."

Sally said, "But won't the food spoil -- " The rest of the sentence seemed to choke and die in her throat. Remembering Gabby's instructions, she realized spoiling was something that didn't belong in the Garden. She paused, took a breath, and began again, "Eve, why would you want to store food when there's more food here than can possibly be eaten?"

"When things are thrown away or wasted, it isn't fulfilling The Creator's purpose. The world won't always have this much food because the animals are going to multiply and fill the earth. When that happens, we will only have enough if we learn how to wisely conserve and use the resources He has given us. Besides, cooked food tastes better, and this is the only place in the Garden where you can cook."

"Where did you get your pots? You haven't had time to make them!"

"My pots come from the same place everything comes from -- the hand of The Creator -- The Father of Lights. He gives us everything we need. From now on though, He expects us to make our own pots and pans. Speaking of work and making things, we'd better get started or we won't be ready when Chippy-Chip and Hoppy return. Sally, dip the pot in the second pool and fill it one-half full."

Remembering her burned feet, Sally asked, "Wouldn't it be better to get cool water from the stream?"

"No! The water in the stream is fresh while the water in the pools is salty. Each pool contains a different amount of salt; the pool furthest to your right is the saltiest. For our stew I think the second pool should be just about right."

It was not long before Hoppy and Chippy-Chip returned with vegetables and nuts. Sally helped Eve cut and place them in the gold pot on one of the hot pools. Eve then sent her to a corner of the room where small plants were growing. This was Eve's spice corner -- lemon grass, licorice, spearmint, pepper and many other spices were there. Sally selected peppers and lemon grass and added them to the stew. Soon a delicious aroma was wafting from the pot. When the stew was done, Eve removed the pot from the hot pool and dished a bowl of stew for Sally.

"*Yum! Yum!*" Sally said as she tasted it.

Laughing, Eve told her, "I know it's good, but I'm not sure *Yum Yum* is a good name. My recipe book will sure be strange with listings like, *Yum! One stew, Yum! Yum! Two stew, Yum! Yum! Yum! Three stew,* and so on, throughout the book."

"The stew tasted so heavenly, *Yum! Yum!* was all I could think of."

"I've got a name -- *Sally's Favorite,*" Eve said, laughing again. "That sounds like a perfect name; I'm going to write it in the book." Saying this, she picked up a porcupine quill and, dipping it in a container of blackberry juice, began to write.

"What else are we going to do?" Sally asked, watching as Eve wrote *Sally's Favorite Stew* in the book.

"I'm in charge of the flowers and also oversee the cleaning of the Garden. Maybe later you can help me clean and arrange but, right now, I have something to ask Adam. Will you please take a message to him?" Seeing Sally nod yes, Eve told her, "Run over to the paper tree and bring me back a sheet of paper. Perhaps after you take my note to Adam, we'll have time to take a tour of the Garden."

"Paper tree?"

"Yes! Here, paper grows on trees. You peel the bark from a paper tree and it comes off in sheets. You can eat the paper, too! Why don't you snack on a piece while you're getting me a small note-sized sheet? You can't miss it. The paper tree is small and has white bark. There's one over there."

Sally, turning to look in the direction Eve was pointing, saw the small white-barked tree. She ambled over and easily peeled off a small, square sheet of the bark. Tearing it in half, she put one piece in her mouth and the other in her pouch for later. As she slowly began to chew the paper, she was pleasantly surprised to find it had a faint peppermint flavor. Looking at the tree trunk, she saw different sized sheets of bark. At the bottom the sheets were wide, while those near the top were narrow. Reaching up, she peeled off a small note-sized sheet.

"Thank you," Eve said, dipping a quill into the blackberry ink. "As soon as I finish writing my note, you can take it to Adam. You'll probably find him in the Command Room. You get there by taking the same opening in the hedge as Bobby did." A few minutes later she folded the note, handed it to Sally, and said, "Hurry!"

Sally rapidly trotted through the hedge, past the peach trees and into a long corridor. At the end of the corridor was a large room that had stone benches along one wall. Bobby and Adam were working on the far side of the room. She ran to them.

CHAPTER ELEVEN

When Bobby left Eve and Sally to join Adam, he walked through the hedge opening, down a corridor, and found he was in a large room with stone benches alongside one wall. Adam, standing near the entrance, greeted him, "Welcome Bobby, are you ready to go to work?"

"I think so! What are all the benches for?"

"There's no way I can get everything done by myself that needs to be done. This is where I hold weekly meetings with my helpers. In fact, there's a meeting scheduled this afternoon. The benches help provide order by keeping the animals from roaming around. This morning I'm here to plan and get ready for the meeting. But, you'll see soon enough," Adam said, walking across the room.

This room, like the others, had walls formed by hedges. The ceiling was the bright, clear blue sky lit by the early morning sun. Bobby, following Adam, glanced at the hedges and saw what appeared to be a yellow pattern woven into them. When he got closer, he saw the yellow pattern was caused by leaves which had been formed into words. The words were arranged in panels high enough from the ground so the words could be easily seen. Bobby read the words on the first panel aloud. *"In the beginning God created the heavens and the earth. And the earth was without form and void and darkness was upon the face of the deep. And the Spirit of God moved upon the face of the waters."*

"Gabby, who wrote these words?"

"The Creator who created everything -- including these writings -- has placed them here. If He doesn't tell us, how else can we learn about our world? How else can we come to know about things that happened before our creation? If God hadn't given us information about our world, we couldn't be good stewards of the Garden. And information about our world is certainly one of the most important things He has shared. If we didn't know better, we might waste time worshiping the sun or moon. But we don't, because He's told us that it's His hand that created them; otherwise, we might offend by worshiping the creation rather than He who created it. Bobby, read the next panel! In it, The Creator tells us the plants in our world are good to eat and that He placed everything in the world for our benefit."

Bobby slowly read the second panel and then glanced around the room. He had been so absorbed in reading the words on the panel that he hadn't noticed what other surprises the room might hold. He saw a large circle on the ground which formed a patchwork of different colors made up of thousands of plants. The outside of the circle was an irregular patch of blue. It completely surrounded the inside which was green, brown, and red. "It looks like a map," he commented.

"It is! It's a map of our world. Do you see the writing at the bottom?"

Bobby took another look and saw the words "*Our World.*" From where he was standing, the words were upside down so it took several moments to read them.

"The small red patch in the center is the Garden. As you can see, we live in a big world."

Bobby, intently studying the map, observed that the red patch was only a tiny part of a large land mass which dominated the world. "It looks like there's only one large continent with the Garden in the center." The ocean was shown much smaller than he had expected. It looked as if all the oceans had been combined into one that completely encircled the land. He thought, *"My science book was right -- at one time the continents were joined together.* He started to mention this to Adam and also to tell him the ocean was too small but his voice choked up and he was unable to speak. "Adam, why do you need a map of the world when you live in such a small part of it?"

"Our job is to transform the entire world so it is like the Garden. It will take many years. This map helps us to plan how to do it."

"It looks like the map is made from living plants."

"It is. As the Garden grows, that allows us to change it whenever we need."

"Are the blue lines rivers?" Bobby asked, pointing to four lines running into the red patch representing the Garden.

"Yes, there are four rivers that come up from the ocean to water the Garden: the Tigris, the Euphrates, the Pishon, and the Gihon. They make the Garden a wonderfully fertile spot."

Bobby thought he hadn't heard Adam correctly. "Did you say rivers run *up* from the ocean? Rivers don't--" Again he was unable to speak. He was trying to tell Adam it was impossible for a river to run uphill.

Not knowing why Bobby seemed puzzled, Adam said, "I see you don't understand the geography of our world. The land is shaped like a large bowl which the ocean completely surrounds. The edge of the bowl is the highest part of the land. Water runs uphill from the ocean through gate-like openings over the high crest and forms four rivers which water the low-lying parts of the land. The rivers are large but, as they branch into streams and give up their water to the land, they become smaller. The plants and trees take water from the streams and, in turn, breathe it out into the sky. In the cool of the evening, this moisture condenses as mist which waters the higher hills. Plants requiring a lot of water are planted on low ground where the streams reach them; however, those requiring less are grown on hills where the mist is sufficient. Now you know why rivers get smaller as they flow up from the ocean."

"Are the rivers salty?"

"Salty? Why should they be salty? Only a few small pools like Eve's cooking pools are salty. That's because their water comes from deep underground where the minerals are. The ocean water is fresh. In fact, it's even fresher than water from rivers which, as they flow through the land, pick up small amounts of salt from the soil. Enough geography for now! If I'm going to be ready for the meeting, I have to get busy. Come, let's go to the next circle."

Bobby went with him. Looking at this second circle, he saw a detailed map with the words "*The Garden*" written at the bottom. To the north he saw where they entered the Garden. The area was labeled, "*The Uncertain Waste Lands.*" At the very center of the Garden was the Tree of Life and the Tree of Knowledge of Good and Evil. He saw another area labeled, "*Command Center*" and knew that this was where he was standing. The southern part of the map showed a series of small rooms. Each room had a picture of an animal in it. "Adam, what are these rooms used for?"

"They've been set up to express the true nature of the animals. You'll be visiting the area soon. During the day most animals roam in the world outside, but at night they return to the Garden to sleep. Bobby, I need your help! Will you please bring me the brown container, red box, and watering can? They're over by that hedge."

Bobby quickly did as he asked. Then Adam carefully opened the brown container and sprinkled the contents on a portion of grass at the bottom of the circle. As Bobby watched, the grass slowly dissolved exposing a bare patch of earth. Next, Adam opened the red box which was filled with small jars. Carefully selecting one labeled "*Essence of Blue Bells,*" he took it out and sprinkled its contents onto the bare patch. Immediately, green sprouts poked their way through the earth and, in less than five minutes, were clothed with leaves and brilliant blue blossoms. "Bobby, take the can and water the plants."

Stooping, Bobby picked up the watering can and poured liquid on the flowers. To his amazement they stopped growing just as fast as they had started.

"The liquid is maintenance juice and comes only from the maintenance plant. There's at least one maintenance plant in every room in the Garden. The juice from the plant's transparent berries stops the growth of any plant it touches. They stop growing and remain the same shape and size."

"What else is the juice used for?"

"Look at the size of the Garden. Without maintenance juice it would be impossible to keep up. You've seen the many hedges. Imagine how much work it would take to trim them every week. We trim every hedge to the shape and size we want only once -- then apply the juice. Thereafter, we only apply the juice once a year for maintenance. When we want to rework a hedge to change its shape or make it grow, we do so by sprinkling it with a special growth juice. Using the special juices God provides us, we have more than enough help to keep the Garden in shape. It even allows us time to plan and expand the Garden." Adam stopped talking for a moment but continued working on the black patch of earth. "We even use maintenance juice on fruit trees. That way they stay the size we want. When we pick the fruit, it all grows back by the next day."

"What are you doing with the patch of earth?"

"Designing plans for a wetland for the ducks, geese, swans, and other waterfowl. At the present time we have no wetland in the Garden for the waterbirds; therefore, they don't feel entirely at home with us. Since the wetland is still in the planning stage, I'm attaching it to the circle with dotted lines. Once we build the wetland and it becomes a permanent part of the Garden, I'll erase the lines."

Adam added some small thin plants to the patch and told Bobby they represented reeds for the marshy areas. He next criss-crossed the area with several streams and large pools of water. Taking some large plants and flowers, he added a meadow and several clusters of trees. When he was finished, he asked Bobby to sprinkle it with maintenance juice. Pleased with his work, he exclaimed, "That's it! The plans for the wetland are almost complete. I still have to come up with a plan to control the water temperature but that shouldn't take long. Maybe I'll ask the beavers to help me with them. And, I might decide to add some finishing touches. But for now, I'm satisfied."

Bobby, hearing a noise, looked up and saw Sally walking toward them. "Adam, here comes Sally. I wonder what she wants?"

CHAPTER TWELVE

Ignoring Bobby, Sally walked directly to Adam. "Here's a note from Eve."

Adam took the note, quickly read it, then smiled. "Eve has asked me to tell the mammoths -- Jumbo and Jumba -- they're to bring their own snack to the meeting this afternoon. If they don't she's afraid she won't have enough refreshments."

"How much does a mammoth eat?" Bobby asked. "Everything I've eaten here has been so good . . . and it appears there's food everywhere. Even if the animals did nothing but eat, it still doesn't seem possible there wouldn't be enough!"

"Oh, there's plenty of food. Eve just doesn't want the mammoths to eat one of our table hedges as a snack. They've done so before and we had to replant it. Because of their huge size, the mammoths tend to think they're more important than other council members. They aren't the least bit sensitive to the needs of others and seem to think everyone was created solely to cater to their comforts, needs and tastes. They don't mean to but, frequently, they blunder around and are destructive. I'd better send Eve's message right away."

Just then two small birds, black with white throats, darted from a nearby hedge and flew to Adam. "No, faithful swifts, I can't use you this time. My message is too long and too heavy for you to carry."

He looked at Sally who was standing beside him shuffling her feet and bobbing her head up and down. "Swifts are fast and are excellent messengers for carrying short messages like *yes, no* or even *come quickly*. But, for long messages, I use Mike-na birds and, for really long messages, I use parrots because they enjoy talking so much. Unfortunately, I can't use parrots for important messages because sometimes they garble the words. Mike-na birds are my best and most reliable messengers since their memory is so fantastic and their speech so clear. I'm always sure my words will arrive exactly as I send them."

While Adam was talking, the children watched as two large blackbirds with white trim and bright yellow bills flew down and landed at his feet. Bobby, who had seen pictures of many different species of birds, thought they resembled large jungle mynas.

As soon as they landed, Adam began speaking. "Mike-na, I want you to take a message to Jumbo and Jumba in the North Meadow. Are you ready?" The two birds made strange whistling noises and then quietly waited for the message. "Jumbo," Adam began, "I want you to bring four bales of hay snacks when you come to the council meeting this afternoon. And, if Jumba comes with you, she should also bring four bales."

He turned to the children. "I want them to bring North Meadow hay because it's so sweet and nutritious. It's full of vitamins and minerals and contains over twenty percent protein. It's good for them and I know how much they enjoy it."

The children listened as Adam finished the message, "Jumbo and Jumba you'll only have time to pick the bales and have a quick snack so don't waste time in the meadow or you'll be late for the meeting. That's it. Mike-na, will you please repeat my message!"

"Jumbo, I want you to bring..." came from the bird's throat. When Mike-na spoke, it sounded as if Adam, himself, were speaking. The bird mimicked his voice perfectly, the same tone, the same pitch. It was like listening to a tape recording.

"Very good, Mike-na," Adam said when the bird finished. "Fly swiftly, and when you're done, come back, because I may have other messages." The birds flew high into the sky, circled once, and then flew north toward the meadow.

A short time later, a flickering blue light near the top of the hedge caught Bobby's eye. "What does the flashing light mean?"

"Look at the map," Adam told him.

Bobby observed a blue light flickering on it, too. "It looks like the light is coming from the animals' rooms in the south end of the Garden," he said. "The light on the map is shaped like an ostrich!"

"That's right! It is an ostrich. A flashing light is part of our warning system. It lets us know when and where there is a problem. This particular light is telling us the ostriches need help. They're always getting into trouble. Usually it's nothing serious, but we still have to check on them. Come on, let's go find out what their problem is and then eat lunch. Look, the sundial says it's nearly noon."

Bobby knew a little about sundials. In fact, he had even made a small one for his back yard. He looked around but didn't see a sundial. Suddenly, he realized the room itself was a large one. He saw, in the main hedge encircling the room, pale green numbers outlined in darker green leaves. He also noticed that the room was round, like a clockface. Looking closer, he saw a shadow pointing at the number twelve. It was almost noon. He was so fascinated by the sundial room that he wasn't aware the others were leaving him behind. He ran to catch up; afraid, if he lost sight of them, he would be lost and unable to find his way. Rushing, he reached the doorway of the Command Room just in time to see them enter another corridor. By the time he finally caught up to them, he was panting heavily, completely out of breath.

Even though he had studied the Garden map just that morning, Bobby was still unfamiliar with most of if. For the next half hour they traveled through a maze of corridors, finally coming to a room having two ostrich-shaped hedges as an entranceway. As they entered, they saw a large male ostrich running frantically around the room. The female ostrich was near the wall with her head poked into a hole in the ground. They could hear her muffled moanings. It took several minutes for Adam to sufficiently calm Mr. Ostrich down so he could ask him what the problem was. The trouble was simple -- too much curiosity on the part of Mrs. Ostrich led them to their present difficulty. Ostriches have a keen sense of hearing. It seems Mrs. Ostrich heard strange noises coming from a room several doors away and felt she would be able to hear them more clearly if she stuck her head in one of their listening holes. When she tried to pull her head out of the hole, she found she couldn't, she was stuck.

Adam walked over and knelt down beside Mrs. Ostrich. "She's not in any danger. The listening holes are all connected so she's getting enough air." With strong fingers he began removing the earth around her head. It took at least five minutes for him to locate the problem -- a root growing through the listening hole had narrowed its opening. "Bobby, please go out and look in the hedge on the right for a bluish-green door. When you find it, tug until it opens. That's where we keep our emergency supplies."

Bobby quickly found the door. It was formed by a network of vines which easily swung open as if on hinges. In the hollowed out space were a number of cannisters. The largest was labeled, "*Maintenance Juice*," and behind it was a red cannister marked, "*Root Cutter*." He was sure this must be the one Adam wanted so he picked it up. Then, seeing several bristle brushes, he chose a medium-sized one and returned to Adam.

Adam dipped the brush into the rust-colored liquid and carefully brushed it onto the root. Immediately, the root began to shrivel and, in a few moments, it was gone.

Mrs Ostrich popped her head out of the hole. Mr. Ostrich, who was still frantically running around, strode up, "Well, what did you hear?"

Adam laughed; then said, "Another emergency taken care of. I hope there aren't any more today. Now, let's hurry back and enjoy the lunch Eve is preparing."

Hearing the word *lunch* made the children realize how hungry they were. The closer they got to the kitchen, the faster they walked. It took them the same amount of time to return as it did in coming but, somehow, it seemed longer. With every step, they felt hungrier and hungrier. Finally, they arrived at the kitchen.

Adam, seeing Eve standing near two bubbling pots said, "I got the note you sent with Sally, and I asked Mike-na to carry it to Jumbo and Jumba."

"Thank you. I appreciate it -- you know how those loveable mammoths like to eat. Speaking of eating, are you here for lunch?" Eve teased. "I thought you were going to be so busy you might not return until supper. Looks like I was wrong -- here you are early and begging for lunch. Which would you like," she asked, pointing at the bubbling pots, *"Sally's Favorite Stew* or *beef stew?"*

"Beef stew!" Bobby exclaimed.

"Me, too," Sally echoed.

It's unanimous," Adam added. "I'll have a bowl, too."

"You'll like it. I made it with fresh beef plant. I'm sure you've seen it in the garden. It's a tan and white vegetable with fuzzy skin. Knowing what it looks like, do you still want some?"

Bobby's adventuresome spirit and curiosity made him say, "Yes!" Secretly he was concerned about how it would taste.

"Adam, will you please thank The Creator for our food," Eve asked.

Adam prayed a beautiful prayer. He spoke as if he were talking to a close friend. After he finished, Eve commented, "The Creator continually watches over us, hearing and seeing everything we do. Every day we take time to meet with Him to seek His advice on the problems of the day. It is right for us to meet and thank Him for this wonderful Garden and for providing our every need." As she spoke, she dished out bowls of steaming stew.

Bobby tentatively tasted his and exclaimed with surprise, "Why, it tastes just like real beef stew!"

"What did you expect it to taste like?" Sally teased. For she knew what he was trying to say -- that it tasted the same as beef stew made from meat.

"It tastes like real beef," Bobby replied, dipping his spoon into the bowl for more. For a while, as everyone ate, there was total silence.

"What should I do with my dish?" Sally asked. She was finished eating, but Adam and Bobby decided to have seconds.

"Throw it in the stream," Eve told her. "We throw away our lunch dishes."

Sally thought it was strange but did what she was told and tossed her bowl in the stream. For almost a minute she watched as it floated away. At first nothing happened; then the bowl vanished in a swirl of bubbles. One moment it was there -- the next it was gone.

Seeing her surprised look, Eve told her, "There's no litter in the Garden. Anything that doesn't dissolve, we carefully wash and put away."

While they were talking, Adam and Bobby finished their second bowl of stew. "Bobby, come with me. We're running late and have to hurry. Staying for a second bowl has caused us to take a longer lunch hour than I had planned." Saying this, he stood, threw his bowl in the stream and left the kitchen. Bobby did the same, following close behind.

CHAPTER THIRTEEN

When Adam and Bobby reached the Command Room, Bobby noticed that a few animals were already there. First he saw Jumbo and Jumba, the mammoths, surrounded by the eight bales of hay they had brought. Then he saw two badgers, two beavers, two owls, a black stallion, and a falcon.

"Not every animal living in the Garden is on the council," Adam told him, "only those in charge of important functions. For example, owls are in charge of the night watch, while falcons are in charge of keeping watch by day. The badgers are master diggers and in charge of excavation. And, as you know, the beavers are in charge of waterworks. The mammoths and horses share transportation duties."

"What time is the meeting supposed to start?"

"Watch the sundial. When the hour hand reaches two, we'll begin. Not all of the council members are here yet. But that doesn't matter because we always start on time, even if they're not here. If we don't start on time, nothing ever gets accomplished. Some of the animals don't seem to have an awareness of the passage of time."

In the distance Bobby saw Gabby walking toward him. When he got close he said, "Hi Gabby! Are you a member of the council?"

"Don't you remember . . . Tyrannosauruses are keepers of the knowledge of the Garden! We attend every meeting in case our knowledge is needed. Yes! Yes! Indeed!"

Two dogs ran in and joined the other council members. "What department are the dogs in?" Bobby asked.

"In your world dogs are known for loyalty and friendliness. Yes! They are! Here, before sin came, you couldn't find a dog that was mean. No! You couldn't! In fact, the dogs are so friendly, they're in charge of hospitality. Yes! They make sure everyone has a friend to sit with. Yes! Yes! They do!"

Shortly before two o'clock, there was a commotion as more animals, including two large dragons, entered. What caught Bobby's attention was a large swarm of flies that flew in with them and landed on a hedge. Surprised, he said, "I didn't think flies would be allowed in the Garden."

"Flies love to live in filth in your world, and are considered pests. Yes! Yes! They are! That's why one of the Evil One's names is Beezelbub, Lord of the Flies. But here, in the Garden, you're in a completely clean world where flies have discipline. Everything in this world is like the fruit -- nothing can spoil! No! No! It can't! Can you guess why the flies are here? Think! If you were going to assign them a responsibility, what would it be?"

"I think I'd have them be an alarm clock. Their responsibility would be to buzz everyone and tell them it's time to wake up. But then again, because I hate alarm clocks, maybe I wouldn't. At home I always shut the alarm off and go back to sleep."

"You couldn't shut off a fly's alarm. Oh! My! No!" Gabby laughed. "If being an alarm clock was all they had to do, they wouldn't be very busy. No! No! They wouldn't! Actually, they serve an important function; they're part of the cleaning department. With their extremely keen eyesight, they can spot even the tiniest of food crumbs left behind by the animals. Yes! They can! They pick up and eat these crumbs until they're full. Any excess they can't eat, they fly to a dump waste pool near the *Uncertain Wastelands* where you burned your feet. The pool takes the nutrition in the crumbs and slowly feeds it to the streams watering the Garden. In that way, nutrients are used over and over again by the trees, flowers and animals."

Sally enterd just in time to hear Adam call the meeting to order. No sooner had he done so, than Jumbo stood and began speaking in a trumpet-like voice. Adam interrupted him, "I'm sure you have many weighty opinions to share, but you're going to have to wait your turn. If everyone talks out of turn, we won't complete our business. Mr. Dog, I recognize you as the first speaker. You have the floor!"

Mr. Dog yapped a friendly greeting, then looked seriously at the council members. "I suggest we discuss the possiblity of guests coming to our Garden. Actually, in a way, all of us are a bit like guests because none of us have lived here very long. But, I ask you to think about guests that may come here in the future. The Garden has so many different paths, corridors and rooms it would be extremely difficult for guests to find their way around. I know that sometimes, even with my good nose to guide me, I still get lost. I propose that we need signs in the Garden."

"Mr. Dog, that's an excellent idea," Adam said. "Eve, would you be willing to help me make signs?" Seeing her nod *yes,* he continued. "Eve and I will make the signs if you'll see that they're installed."

"Signs won't help on a dark night," Mr. Owl spoke up. "What can we do to help them find their way at night? During the day they'll have signs and guides, but whoo, whoo will help them at night? Even if they can't fly, maybe they could follow me."

Jumba, the mammoth, stood. "Any animal with any sense sleeps at night. We won't need guides at night!"

"Maybe we could use the cats. They have excellent night vision," Mr. Owl continued, as if he hadn't heard Jumba's trumpet voice. "We want every guest to be comfortable -- not only the day lovers but also lovers of night. Nights are beautiful, cool, and serene. And it's the only time you can see the stars."

"You're right, Mr. Owl! Why, sometimes even a day lover enjoys going out at night to look at the stars," Mr. Dog yapped. "Maybe we could make arrangements for lights. Do you think the fireflies would be willing to help? We know how well they fly in formation. Maybe they could form an arrow pointing the way in, and an exit sign showing the way out. I make a motion that we ask the fireflies!"

His motion was voted on and unanimously passed. The fireflies would be asked to serve as night lights in the Garden. Mr. Owl, Head of the Night Watch, was put in charge to ask and direct them. With his acute night vision, he would fly ahead of the fireflies and wait for them to catch up.

The next item -- building the wetland -- was the main item on their agenda. Adam began, "The ducks tell me the waterfowl need ponds, reeds and marshy grounds for when they start to raise families. Right now, they're getting by, but when their families arrive, the need will be critical. I've drawn up a tentative plan for the wetland on the Command Room map. Many of you have stated you feel this project should be given a high priority. There are several things we must consider, but the first should be to decide what to do with the dirt we dig up when building the wetland."

"I don't think we should carry it very far," Jumbo grumbled. "I'd place it outside the Garden near the wetland. We could pile it into a large mound." Adam allowed him to speak freely since most of the heavy lifting and carrying would be done by him and Jumba.

"What are we going to do with such a large mound of earth?" Mr. Dog whined.

"If we pile it high enough, then maybe from the top we could see the entire Garden," said Mr. Falcon. "When I'm flying high above the Garden, it's absolutely stunning."

"Maybe we could turn it into a tourist attraction," Mr. Dog yipped excitedly.

Mr. Badger didn't go for the idea. "I doubt it! There won't be enough dirt to make a mound high enough to see the entire Garden. Mr. Beaver, do you agree that most of the ponds and waterways will be quite shallow?"

"Yes, they will. I recommend we place the dirt right next to the wetland. That's more sensible and will take far less work. It doesn't matter how large the mound is, we should still try to make use of it.

Perhaps, if the otters help, I could construct slides going down to the water for them to play on. If we work hard, we might even build tunnels to bring water to the top so the slides become water slides. I'm sure that the waterfowl, water creatures and their children will enjoy having such a nice place to play. If you want, I'll put my engineering mind to work and come up with a plan."

"Mr. Beaver, that sounds like an excellent way to dispose of the dirt," Adam said. "Will someone make a motion that we use the extra dirt from the wetland to make water slides?"

Mr. Otter made the motion. It was seconded by Mr. Bear and brought to a vote.

A loud chorus of *Ayes* filled the room.

"Good," Adam said, "now we should decide when to begin construction. I think our current plans are sufficient in detail to start excavating. If necessary we can add more details later."

After additional discussion, they unanimously voted to meet the next morning shortly after sunrise to start work on the wetland.

Next, Adam asked, "Does anyone have any problem they want to bring before the council? This is the time for new problems and business."

"I'm not sure if it's a problem or not," Jumba began. In spite of her large size, she was shy and didn't like to be conspicuous. "As I was picking my bales of hay in the North Meadow--" She stopped talking and looked hungrily at her remaining two bales. She had eaten her other two as a snack and it still wasn't time for refreshments. "Well," she continued, "as I was passing the large orchard beside the meadow, I noticed what appeared to be broken branches in one of the apple trees. I was quite a distance from the tree so I'm not positive if the limbs were actually broken. But, if they were, why would someone do something like that -- who would want to break a tree's branches?"

"I think we should immediately verify what Jumba has told us, to see if she's correct," Adam said. "This could mean we have a serious problem. Swifts, go investigate and bring us a report as quickly as you can! While you're gone, the rest of us will take a refreshment break." The swifts, obeying Adam, flew from a hedge and winged their way toward the North Meadow.

Eve brought them some soft, green-skinned fruit. The children didn't know what it was but found it tasty and very juicy. Before they finished eating, the swifts returned to the Command Room and landed near Adam, saying, "What Jumba has told us is true." They confirmed that, indeed, the apple tree in the orchard had broken branches.

This news excited the birds, insects, and animals; it took several minutes for Adam to get the council to come back to order. In small groups the question went around and around the room, "What does this mean?" They were puzzled because, in their limited experience, they had never heard of anything like this happening before. It was beyond comprehension that someone, or something, would want to destroy a perfectly good tree.

Adam asked Gabby, the keeper of the true knowledge of the Garden, to come forward and speak. Upon arrival, he shared his knowledge, "It's not hard to explain the broken branches. No! No! It's not! It simply means Evil is loose. Evil is always self-centered and doesn't care what damage it causes. Whenever or wherever you find wanton damage, you know it indicates Evil. Yes! But our Creator is greater than any evil! Yes! Yes! He's greater! As long as we follow Him, the Garden can't be harmed. Even though Evil may walk in the Garden, as long as you're following God, you're under His protection and Evil cannot effect or harm you. No! It can't! You truly are protected! It's important you know and remember this. Yes! Yes! Very important!"

"We'll protect the Garden!" the dragons growled boldly.

"I know you're strong and brave, but don't ever underestimate the power of Evil. When Evil threatens, size and bravery may not help. And, remember, pride is a dangerous thing to have when you're dealing with wrong. Yes! It is!"

Wanting to think about what Gabby told them, Adam dismissed the council. When they broke up, it was as if a dark shadow had fallen across the beauty of the Garden.

CHAPTER FOURTEEN

Late that evening, after running several errands, Gabby came to talk to the children. "If you're not too sleepy, how would you like to go on a nighttime jaunt?" Not waiting for an answer, he continued, "The fireflies are anxious to try out their new guest lighting maneuvers and want someone to practice on. Yes! Yes! They do! You're doing good. So far no one knows you're really guests from the world that will be. You've done well fitting into life in the Garden. Yes! Yes! You have!"

"I love it here. It's fun having animal friends to talk with," Sally said. "I wish I could stay here for a long time. Everything I've seen and done has been neat. I even told Eve the next project for the Garden should be the construction of a children's nursery. She told me she thought it was a great idea, but she'd have to talk to Adam about it. I suggested that the hedges around the nursery be trimmed like dolls and -- "

"I'm afraid that conditions in the Garden will change soon. When that happens, then we'll see if you still love it here. Yes! We will! But, for now, continue to enjoy the Garden's beauty. It's always right to enjoy God's gifts. Yes! Yes!"

Bobby joined in by declaring, "I'm not a bit sleepy -- I feel like I could stay awake all night! Gabby, where are you going to take us?"

"Don't tell us," Sally said. "Keep it a secret."

Looking down at their eager faces, Gabby laughed. "I'll keep it a secret. Yes! Yes! I will! But let's get started and not waste any more time talking. Soon it will be dark enough for the fireflies to start practicing."

The moon had not yet risen, making the brilliantly shining stars appear so close it seemed they could reach out and touch them.

Though brilliant, their soft light barely gave off sufficient light for them to follow Gabby. It was as dark as that time when, just before dawn, mists roll in, partially obscuring the landscape.

Soon Bobby spotted a long string of fireflies flying toward them with their small yellow tail lights blinking on and off. As they watched, the fireflies formed the shape of an arrow which pointed straight ahead. Something was odd, but he wasn't sure what it was. Then, he realized that, like a long string of Christmas tree lights, they were blinking on and off in unison. He watched the arrow dart forward a short distance, then fly further ahead. Suddenly they burst into many small points of light, and the blinking words, NORTH MEADOW replaced the arrow. The letters were joined together as if written by a giant hand in cursive script. Suddenly the base of the N streaked away and the rest of the words unraveled letter by letter and disappeared. Bobby immediately understood that the fireflies were indicating that this was the direction to go to get to the North Meadow. Walking in the direction the fireflies pointed, they entered a room and saw that, once again, the fireflies had formed a long string of blinking lights.

"I think they're doing a fine job, don't you?" Gabby asked.

"They're so much fun to watch I'm afraid I might forget to look where I'm going and run into a bush or something," Bobby replied. "But I wouldn't miss seeing this for anything."

Once again, the blinking lights took the shape of an arrow and broke apart, reforming themselves into the words COMMAND ROOM. This process was repeated through several more rooms until finally they flashed NORTH MEADOW. Gabby had barely started to thank the fireflies for their service when a strange voice drifted down from above.

"Whoo, whoo are you? ... What do you think Gabby, is that a good way to greet a guest?" asked Mr. Owl, flying down and landing in front of them. Without waiting for a reply, he continued. "I'm your guide this evening! By the way, my name is Whooty, Whooty the Owl."

"Whooty, you scared me," Sally told him. "I think you better find another way to announce yourself or, at the very least, wait until you're seen before speaking."

"You scared me, too," Bobby said. "And that really surprises me because I'm a boy and boys are supposed to be brave."

"I'm sorry I frightened you. I guess I do sound spooky," Mr. Owl chortled, evidently pleased with himself. "But I think a surprise greeting would make things interesting for our guests. Come, follow me!" He began to slowly fly across the meadow. "This is where Jumbo and Jumba picked hay and, just ahead, is the orchard."

Sally didn't know if it was the scary way Whooty had greeted them, or the shadows that appeared to move in the faint light, but she nervously peered at each shadow-- expecting to find it was hiding an ugly, fearful creature. She continuously told herself she wasn't afraid, but she was! Once they left the Garden, she was even more apprehensive. And the deep darkness under the trees didn't do a thing to help. *It feels as if something evil is watching us!* she thought. *I wonder if it's the Serpent?* Then Whooty, flying ahead of them, disappeared into the trees.

"Once you've been in the Garden, you're aware whenever something isn't right. Yes! Yes! You are! You've seen evil in your world and know the trouble it causes. Not long ago the Evil One was here in this very place. But he's no longer here. No! He's gone! What you feel is the lingering effect of his presence."

Bobby talked about this effect. "In the Garden it feels as if the entire earth is happy and in harmony. But here, there's a sadness in the air."

"That's a good description. Yes! Yes! It is! See the broken branches in the tree ahead. There, at that place, the feeling will be even stronger. Yes! It will! It's always stronger where the Evil One has done damage."

As they approached the damaged tree, Sally shuddered. "It feels awful! Let's go back!"

"We won't linger because this isn't what we came to see. No! No! It isn't! This just happened to be on the way."

"Whoo, whoo! Where are you? I've been flying as slowly as I can. Hurry, and this time try to follow me more closely," Whooty said from his perch on a rock. As they approached, he flew off ahead of them.

Bobby marveled at how quietly Whooty flew. Even with his sensitive Tyrannosaurus hearing, he heard no sound as the owl glided through the trees. This time, while Whooty wound his way in and out through the trees, they managed to stay close. The owl changed directions so often that Bobby was soon totally lost. He admitted that, even if it were daylight, he would probably still have a difficult time finding his way back. After walking for what seemed a long time, but actually was only about half an hour, they came to a clearing. Once again Whooty called, "Whoo, whoo, we're here! It's just ahead! From here you should be able to find the way without me. All this flying has made me tired and hungry so I'm going to stop to eat and rest for a while. I'll be back for you in about an hour."

Entering the clearing, they saw a sliver of moon had risen and, while it wasn't very bright, it did help them to see a distance away. Flickering shadows were moving around a fire. Immediately Bobby knew what was causing the shadows. "Dragons, those are dragons!"

"Right! This is why we're here. Yes! It is! We've come to visit the dragons. While you're here with them, you can say anything you want to about your world. You don't have to hide anything; they know who you really are. Yes! Yes! They do!"

"Aren't the dragons followers of the Evil One -- enemies of man?"

"Oh! Dear me! No! No! That's not true! Many dragons faithfully served God until their kind died out and became extinct. But enough about that; let's join them. We don't have much time!"

"Greetingss, friendss Bobbys, Sallys, ands Gabbys," they heard a low rumbling voice say. Each word spoken ended in a hiss. "Welcomes tos thes dragons frolics."

"How come we can now understand what they're saying when earlier we couldn't?" Bobby asked.

"Your ears are becoming more in tune with life here. Yes! Yes! They are! You'll find that for every day you spend in the Garden, you'll have better hearing and a greater understanding of all that is happening. Hearing and understanding help lead you to truth. Yes! Yes! They do!"

"Gabbys sayss yous woulds likes tos shares thes custards acorns fruits withs uss tonights," the rumbling hiss continued. "Comes closers."

The children stepped forward until they could clearly see the dragons were sitting in front of a pile of dark red fruit. Each piece of fruit was about the size of a ping-pong ball.

"Takes ones," a dragon commanded.

Bobby, picking up a piece, was surprised at how heavy it was.

"Gives its tos mes," the dragon told him.

When Bobby handed him the fruit, the dragon said, "Watchs mes." The dragon placed the custard acorn on the ground, took a deep breath and gently blew on it. A thin wisp of smoke came from the dragon's mouth. Then a flame burst forth striking the fruit. The dragon continued blowing heat onto the fruit. As Bobby watched, the custard acorn commenced to swell. Soon it was bigger than orange and still growing. In another minute it was bigger than a grapefruit. When the dragon stopped blowing, the fruit had grown to the size of a basketball. "It'ss readys nows," the dragon told them.

Bobby picked up the hot fruit and was surprised to find it weighed the same as it did before. Since it was bigger now, he expected it to be heavier-- but it wasn't. It was soft, warm, and fluffy with a color that faded to a pale pink. He ripped it open and put a piece in his mouth. It tasted a little like a roasted marshmallow, only better. It was sweet, mellow and left no aftertaste. Slowly, he ate the rest of it, enjoying every bite. Seeing Sally was also eating a roasted acorn, he asked, "Aren't they good?"

"Theys ares deliciouss, thanks yous," she said, falling into the dragon's hissing speech. They each ate two more and were so full they couldn't eat another bite.

"Whats dos yous thinks ofs creations nows yous ares heres ands cans sees thes truths? a dragon asked them.

"I've learned many of the things which are written about science in my school books are wrong," she answered. "Creation and the beginning are much more wonderful and beautiful than what's described in a book. Most school books don't even mention God or His creation."

"And in science we've been studying the *big bang* theory," Bobby added. "The teacher told us everything in the universe was created by a big explosion."

A dragon sitting next to Bobby spoke. "Dragonss knows alls abouts firess and explosionss. Littles explosionss makes littles messess ands bigs explosionss makes bigs messess. Thes Gardens iss nots as messs. Ans explosions dids nots makes thes Gardens."

Gabby interrupted their conversation. "We've been here almost an hour. Yes! Yes! We have! We have to go! Whooty will be waiting."

Reluctantly, they said goodbye, thanked their new friends, and followed Gabby back to the orchard. Whooty was waiting. "Whoo, whoo, what took so long? I was starting to think I'd have to come and rescue you from the dragons."

Perhaps because they were so tired, the trip back to the Garden seemed longer. When they reached the North Meadow, Whooty left them and they were greeted by the fireflies spelling out, *WELCOMES BACKS GUESTSS.* Bobby shook his head in disbelief. He couldn't believe his eyes. "Gabby, did they take spelling lessons from the dragons?"

"Oh! Dear me! No! Not really! They know we're returning from visiting the dragons and are pretending they're dragons to make us feel welcome."

Gabby noticed the fireflies had added additional flourishes to their routine -- the arrows they formed seemed to quiver in the air. But he was the only one who noticed. The children didn't -- they were too sleepy. They were glad when, at last, they reached their sleeping area.

CHAPTER FIFTEEN

The next morning the children didn't wake until nearly nine o'clock. They had planned on waking earlier so they could watch work start on the wetland project. But, since they had gotten home so late, they overslept and the sun was now shining down on them from high in the sky. Bobby finally opened his eyes and looked around, saying, "This sure would have been a good time to have had a *buzzing fly alarm clock!*"

Hearing his voice, Sally sleepily asked, "Bobby, what time is it?"

"I'm not sure but it must be late because Gabby's already gone, and my growling stomach tells me it's late. I'm starved."

"I'm not; I'm still full from last night. We sure had a good time with the dragons, didn't we? I'd like to go back again tonight and eat more of that delicious fruit."

"I could eat at least three pieces right now. Without a doubt, that fruit is the best I've ever eaten. I like it even more than what used to be my favorite food -- peppermint chip ice cream. I'm sure Gabby probably has an interesting and exciting day planned but all I want is an interesting and exciting breakfast. We may not have custard acorns but I'd settle for a bowl of Eve's beef stew. As soon as we eat breakfast, we should hurry over to where they're building the wetland. I wonder why Gabby didn't wake us to go with him?"

At that moment Gabby entered. "I see you sleepyheads finally woke up. You've almost slept the day away. Yes! Yes! You have! The animals are about to start work. It's fortunate that they're rarely on time or you would have missed it. Yes! Yes! It's taken Adam several hours to organize them. Hurry! Lets go! If we leave right away, we can still get there before they start. Yes Yes! We can!" Seeing the look on Bobby's face, he added, "Don't worry, we'll stop on the way and get you something to eat."

Gabby turned and left as quickly as he had entered. Bobby barely had time to stretch before he had to leave to catch up to him. "Sally, there's one advantage I've found in being a Tyrannosaurus -- I don't have to get dressed. It's really nice to wake up and be ready to go."

"Dressing up is something I really miss. I love wearing pretty clothes. But, when I clean my room, I sure don't enjoy picking them up. There are two things I definitely don't miss -- cleaning my room and making my bed."

Gabby stopped at Eve's pantry where they selected some fruit to be eaten on their way to the construction site. Adam had carefully chosen the site where the wetland was to be created. It was located just outside the southern edge of the Garden. When they arrived, the first thing that caught their eye, was a large crowd of animals. They saw Jumbo and Jumba standing in the middle of the meadow that soon would be transformed into the wetland. They were so tall that they towered above the other animals. Then, seeing Adam near the edge of the meadow surrounded by a smaller group of animals, they went to greet him. He was examining a large pile of wooden poles.

"Those poles come from pole trees," Gabby told them. "They grow in lengths of four, eight, twelve, and fourteen feet and come in diameters of two and four inches. Yes! Yes! They do! Jumbo and Jumba must have carried them here."

"What will Adam use them for?" Bobby asked.

"Watch and see! Yes! Watch and see! Look over to Adam's left and you'll see a large stack of sheetrock. It looks like most of the building supplies are already here. Yes! Yes! It does! Apparently we arrived just in time."

Bobby walked over to the sheetrock and looked at it with interest. It was similar to thin sheets of mica, only larger -- at least four by eight feet. Since the sheetrock was thin, he guessed it probably wasn't very heavy.

A few moments later, a bird flew to Adam with what looked like a piece of rope in its beak. "That's twine from the twine vine. Yes! Yes! Any size string or rope can be obtained from the twine vine -- there's a kind and size available for any purpose. Yes! There is!"

Adam selected three twelve-foot poles and was busy instructing the woodpeckers where to drill holes. Following his instructions, the woodpeckers drilled and, when they were finished, the racoons came to help Adam tie the poles together. They watched and, once they saw how he wanted them tied, took over and completed the job. Adam then selected three more poles for the woodpeckers to drill and the racoons to tie. When the two bundles were completed, he joined them together using a dozen shorter poles to form the framework of a cart.

While he was inspecting the newly constructed cart to make sure it was solid, two horses trotted up. On their backs they carried two huge bean pods from the round jungle bean. After the racoons and badgers unloaded the pods, Adam turned to one of the large red-headed woodpeckers and said, "Woody Pecker, open these for me!"

The woodpecker flew over and, just as Adam had asked, split them open. As the pods split apart, two large flat beans, each at least two feet in diameter, fell to the ground. Next, Adam asked Woody to drill a hole in the center of each of the beans so they could be used as wheels for the cart. After attaching the wheels, he asked some of the animals to help lift and tie the sheetrock on the cart. While the animals worked, Woody jokingly complained that drilling the holes had dulled his bill and he would have to get it resharpened.

"Rhino, come here! We're ready to dig," Adam called to the rhinoceros. "Start cutting the meadow into strips." The children had previously seen the rhinocerous from a distance but never this close. It was huge. They noticed there was a large horn rising from the front of its snout which came to a sharp point on top. Hearing Adam's command, the rhinoceros lowered its head so the tip of the horn penetrated the ground. Slowly, it began walking toward Adam leaving a line behind it in the meadow grass where its horn had torn the earth. After walking across the meadow, Rhino turned and walked back making a second cut three feet from the first -- dissecting the meadow into strips.

Adam's next order was to the moles and badgers. "Moles! Badgers! Now it's your turn. Get to work!" Immediately the moles started to undermine the strips of meadow grass. The badgers then rolled the long strips of freed grass into large bales. When the bales became so large that they were difficult to handle, they loaded them on the cart. When the cart was full, Jumbo pulled it just beyond the edge of the new wetland and unloaded it.

Once the first section was completely cleared of grass, Adam and Mr. Beaver looked at the building plans. Occasionally, one of them would stop and outline where a pool, stream, or marsh should be. Carefully he marked the ground where these things were to go. He then called every animal that had special paws or claws designed by The Creator for digging, and ordered them to commence excavating the areas.

Late in the afternoon, Eve brought refreshments to them. She was dressed in olive green light that looked almost like old leather. She told them it was her working dress.

"Here, try my new recipe," she said, pouring them a drink. I took water from the soda pool, added strawberries and a little juice from the passion fruit... Oh, yes, I almost forgot, two or three cotton puffs to thicken it. On my way here I stopped and placed the container in a small whirlpool to blend everything together. I haven't named it yet. Do you think you could help me come up with a name?"

As Sally sipped her drink, it left the sensation of strawberry coolness in her mouth. It tasted like a strawberry ice cream soda but with a more delicate flavor. She was going to suggest calling it *strawberry ice cream soda,* but decided it wouldn't be appropriate to give it a name from the future.

"Eve, this is one of the tastiest recipes you've ever made," Adam said. "I think we should name it using the first letter of the alphabet. It doesn't taste like apple or apricot so we can't call it apple or apricot cordial. Let's see. Aa, ab, -- am, -- amb... ambrosia! I like that and it seems to fit. We'll call it ambrosia . . . strawberry ambrosia!"

Finishing his drink, Bobby turned his attention back to the worksite. One of the dinosaurs that he'd nicknamed Dyna Dozer, because of a large scoop on top of its head, was busy using the scoop to pick up large amounts of loose dirt. Then she carried it over to the cart and dumped it. Dyna Dozer was working so fast that Adam had to build a second cart just to keep up. Jumbo continued pulling the first cart and Adam assigned Jumba to the second one.

Under the beaver's supervision, the mound of earth steadily grew. After each load, the beavers would precisely place the dirt and then compact it down with their broad tails.

Unlike Bobby, who was very interested in building things, Sally soon grew tired of the construction work and wandered away. She was fascinated watching the animals work together and would have liked to talk or play with them. But, they were too busy. For a few more minutes she watched the beavers. Then, thinking there might be other animals on the outskirts of the meadow with whom she could play, she walked aimlessly toward the orchard. In minutes she was so far away she no longer could see the meadow or wetland. If she listened closely, she could faintly hear the distant sounds of animals working. As she continued to wander, suddenly, on the path in front of her, she saw a large white lamb. Describing The Lamb as *white* didn't do justice to the dazzling bright purity of its fleece., Taking two steps toward The Lamb, she abruptly stopped, knowing somehow that it wouldn't be proper to go any closer. As The Lamb gazed at her, she saw what appeared to be sparkling lights dancing in its eyes. She felt awkward, as if she should say or do something. "Who? -- Who are you?"

"I Am," The lamb replied in a low majestic rumble. "In peace I am a Lamb. I am watching over My people."

"I've never seen you before -- who are your people? Are you the king of the sheep?"

"You have seen Me," The Lamb corrected her. "You have seen Me in the dancing lights. Now you see Me in another of My names. All are My people. I am King of all."

Sally felt a strong urge to kneel at The Lamb's feet but; instead, bowed her head. "Who are you watching over now?" she asked softly.

"I am watching over you. You should not go further down this path for the Evil One is a short distance away. He is keeping track of what is happening in the Garden, and you are not strong enough to face him by yourself. Go now. Return to the meadow. Fear not, for I am with you."

Sally did not want to leave the beauty of The Lamb but, knowing she had to obey, turned and took a few steps down the path. Then, with a burst of speed, she ran -- ran to the safety of the meadow. When she arrived, she saw work had stopped and Adam was sending the animals home. Quietly she joined Bobby and Gabby to start the long trek back to the Garden. They traveled in silence. It wasn't until they were completely safe in the confines of the Garden that she told them about meeting The Lamb.

CHAPTER SIXTEEN

"Gabby, why don't all of the animals live in the Garden? Yesterday, outside of the Garden on our way to the meadow, I saw dragons living in large caves. And when I checked the map in the Command Room, I didn't find a home listed for Dyna Dozer or any of the other dinosaurs."

"Bobby, that's because the Garden isn't large enough yet to house all the animals. Adam has to enlarge it by adding new features until there's enough room for them. Yes! Yes! He does! For example, once the wetland is finished, it will be used, not only by the ducks and other waterfowl, but also by the hippopotamuses. Yes! It will!"

"But Gabby," Sally exclaimed. "Dyna Dozer, other dinosaurs, and dragons are the only ones I've seen living outside. Is it because they're so large, or do small animals live there, too?"

"Let me think! Oh! Dear me! Yes! Yes! One small animal that immediately comes to mind is the hedgehog. The hedgehogs find our beautiful hedges too appetizing to resist. Why, if Adam allowed them to live here, in less than half an hour they would seriously damage many of the Garden's walls. Yes! Yes! They would! It's better for them, and us, that they live outside where they can eat as many scrub plants as they want. Remember, The Creator has given Adam dominion to rule over every living thing: the birds that fly in the air, the creatures that live on land, the fish that live in the ocean. Yes! Yes! Adam has dominion! At this time the Garden doesn't extend to the ocean so everything living in the ocean is technically living outside. However, not far away, there is an inlet that comes in from the ocean. Yes! Yes! There is! Adam has told me the wetland work is going so well he's going to place the beavers in charge and go visit his ocean subjects for the very first time. Would you like to go with him?"

"Hurrah," Bobby shouted enthusiastically. "Count me in! I really enjoy exploring in the water and playing in the sand by the ocean. When do we leave?"

Sally teased him. "Bobby, I'm surprised you're willing to leave before breakfast!" But the excitement in her voice showed that she felt the same way about going as he did.

"I'm always hungry!" he responded. "I have a huge body to feed -- a growing body! And, besides, everything tastes so good that I hate to stop eating. Just look at the food in Eve's pantry; there's still many things I haven't tried."

"Well, why don't you two run to the pantry and get some of those good things to eat so we can get started. I promise that before the day is over you'll get a chance to eat something you've never tasted. Yes! Yes! I promise! Hurry now! We have an exciting day ahead! It's at least a two-hour walk to the ocean. Hurry! Adam will be leaving soon. Yes! Yes! He will!"

After breakfast they met Adam, who led them through flowery meadows and luscious orchards, as they trekked slowly upward over low rolling hills toward the ocean.

"Were you afraid when you saw The Lamb?" Bobby asked.

"Not afraid, but I sure was scared. It was a scared kind of afraid. I'm not sure if I can explain it. If I were Gabby, I'd say, 'Oh! Dear Me! I hate to explain! Yes! I do! I do!' I'm not Gabby but I'll try and tell you what it was like. If a tiger were chasing you -- because you know what's going to happen if he catches you -- you'd feel the afraid kind of scared. But if you saw something magical, like a fairy, you might feel scared but not be afraid -- because you don't know what the fairy is going to do! It was more like that kind of fear: the fear of facing the unknown, something great and powerful. It was the kind of fear a person experiences when they meet someone important."

"I wish I could have been with you. I would have liked to have seen Him, too."

"Bobby, you have seen Him. He told me He was in the dancing lights."

"I know, but I also want to see Him as The Lamb. You sure had an exciting adventure! I guess I'm just feeling sorry because I wasn't with you."

"Your day was thrilling, too. Here, in the Garden, every day is an exciting surprise."

Bobby agreed.

Time passed swiftly. It seemed they had barely started to talk when Gabby interrupted. "We're almost there! Yes! Yes! We are! The ocean is just over the top of this hill."

Adam, who was a short distance ahead, disappeared over the crest of the hill. They hurried to catch up. Reaching the spot where they last saw him, they heard a large splash which was followed by a spray of water similar to a geyser shooting high in the air. Gabby laughed. He was taller and could see what was happening. "That was the porpoises giving Adam a twenty-one splash salute."

As soon as they stepped over the crest, the soil abruptly changed to fine white sand. The ocean was much nearer than expected -- not more than ten feet away. Adam was standing at the edge of the ocean, and a large group of porpoises formed a semicircle in the water around him. Bobby, looking into the sky-blue ocean, was surprised by how clear it was. So clear that, for a moment, it seemed as if the sky had dropped down and become the ocean. But, he knew it wasn't the sky because he saw strange sea creatures swimming in the water. There were brilliant-orange sea horses and schools of rainbow-hued fish. Suddenly, one of the schools darted toward Adam, barely skimming the surface. When they were close, they leaped out of the water and, in formation, flew past him through the air. Then they fell back into the ocean without a splash.

Bobby was amazed to see that as they flew through the air, their bodies spelled out, "*WELCOME ADAM.*" "Gabby, that was fantastic," he said, "but tell me, why is the water so clear?"

"One reason is because there's no sea weed. In the beginning there are only gardens in the ocean. Yes! Only gardens! Maybe you'll get a chance to see them later. Another reason is because ocean water doesn't contain salt. No! No! It doesn't! It's as fresh as the clearest mountain stream in your world. There are many other reasons why the water is so clear. Yes! Yes! There are! But those two are the main ones."

"I agree with Bobby," Sally exclaimed, "I've never seen such clear water. I bet everything washed in it comes out sparkling clean. The sand on the bottom is so clean and white -- like patches of snow. But I also see red and brown sand. All together they look like roads on the bottom."

Gabby smiled. "I wouldn't be surprised to discover this water could remove any spot or stain. No! I wouldn't! Even without soap! But the most important thing about the ocean isn't its sand or the clarity of its water; it's that the land animals... Oh! Dear me! I'm so awkward at explanations! Yes! Yes! I am! Lets see... some animals, such as otters and beavers live on land and breathe air but can also live in the ocean and breathe water. It's not quite the same as breathing air. Oh! My! No! They still need to breathe air. But some, like otters, can remain underwater for a full day without surfacing. Even we Tyrannosauruses can breath the water. Of course, not as well as we do air. Oh! Dear me! No! But well enough to stay submerged for up to two hours."

"Gabby, are we going to swim beneath the water and breathe?" Sally asked with anticipation.

"Most of the time we'll travel on the surface. But yes! Yes! We'll spend at least part of the time underwater. The porpoises will be our guides. That's why they've come to greet us. Actually, they'll be more than guides. Yes! Yes! They will! They'll also be our transportation. Because we've so far to go, they're going to let us ride them. We're traveling to the undersea Sand Castle to be with Adam as he meets with his Council of Sea Creatures. Until we get to the area near the Castle, we'll ride on the surface. Yes! We will!"

Adam, mounted on the back of a porpoise, was skimming across the surface of the water. "Come!" Gabby said, walking to the water's edge. "Choose your mount and ride in front of me."

As soon as they entered the water, the two porpoises assigned to be their mounts swam under them. Sally found that the long legs of a Tyrannosaurus were ideal for grasping the porpoise and had no trouble staying firmly seated. As amazing as it was to be riding a porpoise; because of the the wonder of the sights, she soon forgot about it. *This must be how a bird high in the sky sees the world*, she thought, looking at the scenes unfolding below. With bright earth colors of red, yellow and brown, she was sure it must be like the Garden in autumn. *It's beautiful!*.

Because they were enthralled by the sights, time swiftly passed. "Aren't the ferns beautiful," Sally called out. "They move so ..." She had started to say, "They move so gracefully," when suddenly her mount dove. Water rushed over her head filling her eyes, ears and mouth.

Later, when they talked, they agreed riding beneath the water was very pleasant. At first they were startled, but quickly adjusted. Describing the sensation of breathing water was difficult, but they agreed their breathing rate slowed down which made it as easy for them to breath water as air. Gabby told them it wasn't the lack of oxygen that periodically forced them to rise to breathe. No, it was the slow buildup of carbon dioxide in their bodies. If they failed to get rid of it, gradually it would cause them to become more and more tired until, finally, they fell asleep. If that happened, they would remain asleep until brought to the surface for fresh air.

Their underwater trip lasted about five minutes. When they returned to the surface, they found their voices were different -- lower and clearer. Laughing, Sally began to sing and when she was finished said, "This is the only time in my life I will be able to sing baritone. I want to hear how I sound. Bobby, you don't have to sing because you're a boy and, when you get older, you'll probably sing baritone, or maybe even bass."

The porpoises submerged, taking them once again beneath the water. But this time was different. They could clearly hear the porpoises talking. Unfortunately, Gabby hadn't taught them how to speak porpoise or any of the other sea creature languages so they had to ask him to interpret what was being said.

Arriving at the Sea Palace, they saw it was built of many shades of beautiful red sandstone. Gabby told them the sharks were in charge of the Palace. It was their responsibility to keep everything sanded smooth by rubbing it with their rough skin. The children watched as the sea creatures gathered for their meeting. Shortly before it started, an octopus swam to them and served refreshments. They were not sure, but it appeared to be some kind of sea plant sandwich. Trying to eat with their mouths full of water was a novel experience. Bobby tried to force as much water out of his mouth as possible before biting into the sandwich. He found his idea didn't work and he still had a mouthful of water. Finally, he decided to just open his mouth wide and take a bite. Chewing it, he thought, *I've got water in my mouth and don't have any idea what I'm eating, but I don't care; it's good!"*

Then, to their surprise, the octopus swam to the very front of the Sand Castle and called the Council of Sea Creatures to order. It was then they realized that, even though he acted like a servant, he was actually in charge. The children couldn't understand what was being said so, after finishing their sandwiches, they swam around the Castle. Later, Gabby mentioned that one thing discussed by the council was the need to formulate a plan to ensure a plentiful supply of greenish-blue oxygen plants for every part of the ocean. The water creatures were concerned about running out of oxygen.

Suddenly, Sally and Bobby were extremely drowsy and decided to return to the meeting. Shortly after swimming back, the entire room and sea creatures faded into darkness. They had remained in the ocean too long and had fallen asleep. They were totally unaware when the porpoises picked them up and carried them to the surface. Even after breathing fresh air, they still felt groggy. In fact, they were so drowsy they didn't even remember the trip back to the Garden.

CHAPTER SEVENTEEN

The next morning when Bobby and Sally talked about their adventure of the day before, they realized they hadn't seen any empty shells on the ocean floor. The sea gardens, which they passed, contained row after row of sea creatures dressed in gorgeous, brightly-colored shells. They watched as live shells scurried in and out, engaging in what appeared to be some strange business. When Gabby joined them, Bobby asked, "Yesterday, why didn't we see any empty shells on the beach or in the ocean? When I lived by the beach, I used to spend hours picking up empty shells."

"Have you already forgotten that in the Land of the Beginning there is no death? Shells only become vacant when the creatures living inside die. Yes! Here in the beginning, nothing is dead; everything is alive. Yes! It is!"

"What were the graceful seashell creatures in the ocean gardens doing?" Sally asked. "They were so beautiful. It looked as if they were dancing."

"They were feeding on small algae water plants. Yes! Yes! They were! In the ocean, algae used for food isn't allowed to touch the water. If it did, the water would no longer be crystal clear. Instead it would be dark and murky. Yes! It would! Algae grown for eating comes from special factories and is carried to the sea creatures through thin feeding tubes that run under the sand. Did you notice the garden where the shells moved faster? Those were members of the clam clan working together in their pearl-making garden. Yes! To make a pearl, the clam must rapidly move around it as it hardens. If they move too slowly, when it's finished it will have at least one flat side. They're planning on using the pearls to trim the Sand Castle and want them to be perfect."

Sally sounded hesitant. "It -- it seems that when we were swimming around in the Castle, I think I remember seeing a room decorated with pearls. But, I was so sleepy, I'm not sure."

"Adam lives in the Garden. How does he know what's happening in the sea?" Bobby asked. "It seems he'd have to know what's happening there in order to rule over the sea creatures -- just as he does with the land creatures."

"Routine messages are brought to Adam by animals that can live in the water or on land. Animals like the otter and beaver. Yes! Yes! Daytime emergency messages are given by the porpoises or flying fish to the falcon patrol. Nighttime emergency messages are given to the owl patrol by shining plankton, spelling out words the same way as the fireflies do. Falcons fly faster than owls but, because owls can see a night message from a greater distance, it takes about the same amount of time to deliver the message to Adam. Yes! Yes! It does!"

"I understand why a falcon is so fast -- speed enables it to catch its prey." Bobby commented. "But I don't understand why, in the Land of the Beginning, the falcon needs to dive so swiftly. They eat fruit just like the rest of us and don't need speed to catch a meal."

"Bobby, if you were here long enough, you'd discover the answer to your own question. Yes! Yes! You would! Let me tell you why they're so fast. The trees bearing the star apple fruit on which they feed have extremely brittle branches. If they were to land on one of the branches, it would break causing the fruit to fall to the ground and splatter. Yes! Yes! It would! The Creator, in His wisdom, created the falcon so it could swiftly dive from the sky and pluck the star apple fruit without destroying the branch or fruit. God does not destroy. No! No! God does not destroy!"

"Gabby, what about owls?" Sally questioned. "Why do they need night vision?"

"God created creatures to enjoy and live in every type of habitat. Some, as you saw yesterday, He created to enjoy the day. Still others, like the owls, He created to enjoy the night. Yes! Yes! He did! Sally, the owls love to eat the bubble fruit that grows only on bubble trees. During the daytime the fruit is very small, only a tiny lump. But, as soon as the sun sets, it swells until it's nearly as large as a grapefruit. At dawn, when the first rays of sun appear, it once again shrivels in size. Yes! Yes! It does! The owls claim bubble fruit is delightful and tastes best when eaten on a dark moonless night."

"Why do Adam and Eve start so late some mornings and stop so early some afternoons? I've been watching and every day they disappear at those times. I know they go somewhere but I haven't figured out where."

"That's when they meet with The Creator. Every day, either early in the morning or late in the afternoon, they meet with Him to discuss their problems and to seek His wisdom and guidance. Yes! Yes! They do! He gives them solutions for their problems. They know that only through His wisdom can they be good stewards -- good caretakers of the Garden. Yes! Only through His wisdom!"

Satisfied with his answers, the children left to begin another fun-filled day of strange experiences and adventure. Each passing day brought a new opportunity to learn more about the Garden. They watched as the wetland was completed and the ducks and waterfowl moved in. They visited the dragons and, once more, ate their fill of custard acorns. On the way back from the dragons' den, Whooty shared a piece of bubble fruit. They agreed it was delicious, but not nearly as good as custard acorn. One night they stayed up all night and watched the mists roll in and water the Garden. The next day they were exhausted, but quickly recuperated. By the following day, they were again eager to resume new adventures.

Several of their trips lasted more than a day. One was to help Adam tap rubber trees which were over two days walking distance away. They were gone for nearly a week and traveled over one hundred and sixty miles. They knew how far they had walked because Gabby told them a young Tyrannosaurus Rex could walk an average of forty earth miles a day. If Adam hadn't been riding a horse, he never could have kept up.

When they tapped the trees, Bobby discovered the gum came in seven flavors and was very much like the gum he chewed back home. However, there was one problem: as you chewed it, the gum gradually melted. A large gumball would totally dissolve in just a few minutes.

Sally's favorite trip was to a grove of maple sugar trees. When they tapped the trees, in no time at all their cups were full of sweet sap. It was clearer, sweeter, and much better tasting than the maple syrup and sugar back home. It was the best she had ever tasted.

They learned how the animals in the Land of the Beginning lived and ate, and what activities they enjoyed. Gradually, one by one, their many questions were answered. They attended the council meetings and listened to the animals discuss projects -- then watched as those projects were started and completed. Adam's current project was planning the creation of a place where the animals could honor and visit The Creator. Because it was such an important project, he wanted it to be perfect and was spending a great deal of time planning it.

Frequently, Gabby was engaged in Tyrannosaurus-type business and the children were left with Adam and Eve. They enjoyed those occasions and what they learned from them.

On one of those days, Sally was asked by Eve to get some thread from the twine vine for a variegated fig leaf tablecloth she was sewing for the kitchen table hedge. Looking at the leaves to determine what color was needed, Sally couldn't help but admire the large brown and gold leaves. Picking one up she rubbed it against her cheek. It had the texture of felt.

After eating lunch with Eve, Sally left to find the twine vine. She had no trouble locating it. It was just outside the Garden in the grove of trees near the dragons' den. By now she was comfortable, not only in the Garden, but also in the countryside surrounding the Garden. Having traveled this area several times at night to visit the dragons, she had no qualms about being here during the day. The twine vine was draped around the tallest tree in the area, making the tree look as if it were draped with a multi-colored spider web of red, blue and green. Sally didn't waste time and busily engaged herself in picking out the thread she needed. She had gathered a half dozen different colors and was about to leave, when she heard an unusual noise behind her. Listening more closely, she determined it was an angry low-pitched voice. Whoever or whatever it was, was too far away for her to understand what was said. But, from the anger in the voice, whoever it was, was out of place in the Land of the Beginning. Silently, she crept into a large clump of leaves which were woven cocoon-like around the twine vine. Fearfully, she peered out between the leaves.

Coming toward her hiding spot was a strange looking gold and purple Tyrannosaurus, covered entirely with jewels which flashed in the sun. *The Serpent,* she thought. *It has to be him. I wonder if he'll see me!* By this time he was so close she could clearly hear what he was saying. "If I were in charge," he snarled, "things would be different. Imagine putting Adam and Eve in charge. Why, anyone with any sense can easily see I'm far better qualified. In fact, I should have been given a throne in Heaven. This world isn't big enough or important enough for me to rule."

Sally didn't know why, but what he said terrified her. Her entire body began to tremble. Never before had she ever been this scared. It was difficult for a Tyrannosaurus, but she tried to make herself small by crouching down further in her leafy hiding place. Holding her breath, she hoped the Serpent wouldn't see or hear her as he passed by. A minute elapsed -- then two. Each one seemed like an eternity. Finally the Serpent's voice grew fainter. Sally let out a deep sigh of relief. Then, realizing he was heading directly toward the Garden, she was again overwhelmed with terror.

Bravely she overcame her fear and decided to follow the Serpent and find out what he was going to do. She didn't know what that might be but, somehow, she hoped she would find a way to stop him. Or, at the very least, warn the others! Shaking, she crept from the safety of her leafy cocoon. Luckily, as she followed, he didn't pay any attention to the trail behind. *With the Lord's help,* she thought, *and my excellent Tyrannosaurus vision, maybe he won't see me.*

But, only a moment later, she was almost discovered when she loudly gasped. This happened when the Serpent stopped to pull down a tree fern. Muttering, he said, "There that's much better! It's monotonous -- everything is alive and growing. The world needs more dead things -- broken limbs and rotting branches. It needs winter's ice, snow and dead leaves. Bare branches is what I like to see." It seemed to Sally that his jewels flared and flashed even more brilliantly. He continued, "But, as long as Adam and Eve have dominion here that won't happen."

Because he was far ahead and almost out of sight, Sally wouldn't have been able to hear everything he was saying if he hadn't been shouting. Suddenly, as he continued toward the Garden, he became quiet. Afraid of losing sight of him, Sally rushed forward. She wasn't sure how she remained unseen, but suspected it might be because his full attention was focused on whatever the task was that brought him here.

The Serpent stopped at the edge of the Garden and Sally heard him mutter, "My timing is perfect. This morning I watched as Adam left for the ocean. He'll be gone most of the day. That will give me plenty of time." Saying this, he slithered into the Garden.

Once in the Garden, he rapidly walked toward the very center. It appeared to Sally that he had thrown caution away since he no longer even looked for cover.

CHAPTER EIGHTEEN

As Sally followed the Serpent into the Garden, she wondered what she could do. Not far away she heard Eve happily singing a joyful song. Soon the Serpent would reach her. Sally did not know what he was up to but was sure it was not anything good. He was getting closer and closer and in another moment would reach Eve. Looking for someone to help; a short distance away, she saw a huge lion. *That's funny*, she thought. *I don't remember ever seeing a lion in the Garden before.* Since the lion was the only animal in sight, she tearfully rushed up to him. When she got close, she trembled at his fierce appearance. Hearing her approach, the lion turned and faced her. His look caused her fear and trembling to leave -- lights danced in His eyes. She knew then that The Lion was also The Lamb and everything was under His control. Though she heard no sound, His words, "My name is The Lion of the Tribe of Judah," pressed in on her mind. "Just as I watched over you as a Lamb, I also watch over my children as a Lion."

"But, but . . . shouldn't we warn Eve?"

"I am free and so are My children, or they wouldn't truly be My children. Even in paradise it is impossible to escape every trial. Until the Serpent succumbed to temptation and became evil, he was a perfect creature in a perfect environment. Eve, too, must choose what she will do when she faces temptation. The Serpent cannot harm her unless she makes the wrong choice. Sally, I am going to let you hear what the Serpent says because you are here to learn the truth. You are safe -- I will not let you be harmed. It would not be right for you to get hurt here in the Land of the Beginning. Soon, before too many days pass, I will send you back to your own time. Go now and learn! Learn and profit from the truth you see. Remember, temptations only become evil when one forgets My presence. Stay behind the hedge and neither the Serpent or Eve will see you. Remember, I am with you always."

Sally crept up and peeked through the hedge. At first she didn't notice the Serpent because he had made himself smaller and was no longer as terrifying. Compared to The Lion, he appeared gaudy and cheap but was still so horrible that she had no desire to meet him face to face.

The Serpent was approaching Eve, who was enveloped in a pink cloud of light. "Good morning, Eve! Your very presence makes the morning glow." Sally was surprised to hear his voice so pleasant and was repulsed by its false sweetness. It was so different from the angry ranting and raving she heard earlier. *Still,* she thought, *I can detect a hint of anger hiding in those syrupy words.*

Eve laughed, "Mr. Serpent, it seems you've got your facts turned around. It's the beauty of the morning -- the beauty of the world -- that's causing my glow. Isn't this a perfectly gorgeous day that the Lord has made?"

"Ah, but it is you who are marvelous. You who are the fairest part of every morning in the Garden. And to think The Creator is shortchanging you."

"What do you mean?" It was clear from her expression and tone of voice that Eve was shocked. "God has given me more than I need and has created everything in the world for me to enjoy. The warm sun makes the days perfect and the cool nights are wonderful for sleeping. He has provided an endless supply of food. The animals are delightful and make me happy. And I have Adam. Me . . . shortchanged! Certainly not!"

"You are the Queen of the Garden and, with your beauty and talent, you deserve to be. Yet He, The Creator, has limited you. I think that is unfair."

"Limited me?"

"Yes! Didn't he tell you not to eat fruit from a certain tree. My point is clear: He is restricting you, limiting you, not allowing you your due."

"Serpent, you have a way of turning and twisting everything. Out of the thousands of trees in the Garden, the only one He instructed us not to touch or eat the fruit from is the Tree of Knowledge of Good and Evil. And even that one small restriction was placed there for our good. He told us something dreadful would happen if we eat the fruit -- that we will die -- whatever that means."

"Eve, you aren't very sophisticated, are you? After all this time you still haven't learned what the world is really like. There is no such thing as dying or death. You've seen the world -- have you ever encountered death? The Creator lied. Come, look closely at the Tree of Knowledge of Good and Evil. If you do, I'm sure that with your intelligence, you'll see how harmless the fruit is. As I told you before, The Creator has been depriving you of something good."

"I don't understand. How can I doubt the Word of the One who created me?"

"God wants you to grow up and learn to do things on your own so that you're not always depending on Him for everything. He placed the tree in the Garden so you could learn how to be independent. He wants you to learn how to think for yourself."

"That doesn't sound right. You're confusing me."

"Just come with me to the Tree of Knowledge of Good and Evil. When you see it, you'll be surprised how much clearer you will think." The Serpent reached out to take Eve's hand; then, evidently thinking better of it, pulled away. Slowly he went through an opening in the hedge toward the very center of the Garden -- toward the Tree of Life and the Tree of Knowledge of Good and Evil.

Eve hesitated -- then stood and slowly followed. To Sally it appeared Eve was mesmerized, as if she were being pulled against her will. Sally looked at The Lion to see if she should follow. The expression on The Lion's face surprised her, it was an expression of indescribable sorrow. "Go! There is still much for you to see."

Sally looked back to see Eve disappear into a corridor which led to the center of the Garden. She waited, then followed, crouching behind the hedges as she made her way. Stopping about thirty feet from the Tree of Knowledge of Good and Evil, she was close enough to clearly see, and hear everything that was said.

The Serpent was talking, "Eve, I'm telling you, The Creator wants you to grow up, and eating this fruit is the only way you can obtain maturity. Now, use your senses! Look at this fruit! What do you think it looks like?"

"It looks as if it were made from pure spun gold. It's absolutely beautiful. Nothing else in the Garden compares to its beauty."

"See! What did I tell you!" the Serpent triumphantly replied. "The Creator has been withholding the most precious thing in the Garden. He's been shortchanging you! Eating this fruit will add spice to everything else in the Garden."

"Doesn't He have a right to withhold as well as give? I receive pleasure whenever I give one of my animal friends a gift. But, if I always give and never withhold, soon the excitement in giving would be gone. Maybe The Creator is waiting until I'm older before He tells me I can eat the fruit. When I see Him in the morning, I think I'll ask Him." She looked toward the hills beyond the Garden.

Sally, peeking from behind the hedge, saw the Serpent shudder at Eve's words. But his voice didn't betray his feelings; the false pleasantness remained. "No, I don't think it would be wise for you to ask Him. Remember, this is a test He is giving to see if you can reach maturity without His help. This is a choice you have to make by yourself. And I'm sure it will please Him if you make your choice soon. Here, let me help." He startled Eve by reaching up and picking one of the golden fruit but, before she could say a word, he gobbled down the fruit in a single gulp. "Eve, eat some. I assure you, it's most delicious."

"Maybe it's all right for you to eat but that doesn't mean it's right for me. Maybe The Creator didn't forbid you, but He did Adam. And I intend to follow His instructions to Adam."

"You're missing the point, Eve. I just tasted both good and evil so I know what I'm talking about. The fruit not only looks and tastes good but also makes you wise. Why do you think I'm so wise? I'll tell you! My wisdom comes from this fruit -- the tasting of the good and evil it contains." The way he said "evil" made Sally shudder. Eve, however, didn't seem to notice. "Wise! Wise!" he repeated. "Eve, if you eat, you'll be like The Creator, knowing everything there is to know about good and evil."

"But I'm already like The Creator. He told Adam we are made in His image and have dominion over all His creation."

"Wise!" The Serpent repeated. "Instead of being like deprived children and subject to another's whims, you will be grown and can set your own standards and rules. By eating the fruit, I have shown it will not harm you. Look at me. As you can see -- I'm still alive and well. You won't know if The Creator is truly good until you have tasted evil. Remember, eating it will make you wise, much wiser than you are now. Go ahead! Try it!"

Sally turned to The Lion who was lying beside her and saw tears streaming down His face. His words were indelibly imprinted on her mind, "I know what evil is, but I taste and eat only that which is good. I want only good for My children, and for them to follow My example. Good and evil can exist together in knowledge but never in deed. When good and evil are both eaten, the evil will always devour and destroy the good. Good must stand alone if it is to remain good."

Sally watched as the Serpent picked another piece of golden fruit and handed it to Eve. Eve took it and held it close to her face, smelling its fragrance. She looked at it thoughtfully. "Sally," The Lion said, "you have seen enough." Suddenly, an overwhelming tiredness came over her; she closed her eyes, and soon was asleep.

CHAPTER NINETEEN

Sally did not remember how she returned, but did remember a dream-like impression of being gently carried to her room on the back of a Lion which was so soft and silky it felt as if she were wrapped in lambskin. When she awoke, it was early morning and the sun was just beginning to peek over the hedges. Beside her, Gabby and Bobby were still sleeping soundly. Gabby stirred. As soon as he opened his eyes she asked, "Did I have a bad dream or did Eve really eat the forbidden fruit?"

"Oh! Dear me! No! Unfortunately, you weren't dreaming, she did eat it. Bobby saw Adam eat some, too."

At the mention of his name, Bobby opened his eyes. "I don't know very much about what happened. Adam and I were returning from a visit to the Sea Palace. It was quite late, already dark. Eve met us on the road carrying a piece of golden fruit. She told us it came from the Tree of Knowledge of Good and Evil and had been given to her by a serpent. She had eaten a piece because he had told her it would make her wise. Eating the fruit, she discovered that it had a marvelous taste and what he had told her was true. She insisted Adam take a bite because, since eating the fruit, she had been experiencing totally new thoughts and sensations.

Adam didn't say anything but looked at her sadly. Then, after what seemed a long time, he took the fruit from her and ate it. What happened next was very strange. I had looked away for a moment and, when I looked back, they were gone -- disappeared -- at least I couldn't see them. You know how, because of their bright glow, you can see them clearly at night -- even from a distance. Well, I was less than twenty yards away, and one moment their light was there and the next it was gone. Snuffed out! There was only darkness, a darkness more intense than any I had ever seen. It was so dark Gabby came and helped me find my way back."

"Gabby, how did I get back? Did you help me, too? I can't remember!"

"Oh! No! I wasn't the one who helped you. No! I wasn't!"

"What Adam and Eve did was wrong," Sally continued soberly. "They disobeyed God, didn't they? Eve seemed to want to please The Creator... I think it's so sad. What will happen now? The sun is shining and everything looks the same but I feel a sense of depression -- of gloom." She could not forget the tears streaming down the Lion's cheeks.

"Sally, Eve didn't have any experience with lying. No! No! She didn't! Everyone spoke only truth to her so she didn't have the necessary knowledge or skills to tell a lie from the truth. She knew that, at times, the Serpent's words didn't sound quite right but couldn't imagine someone intentionally not telling the truth. Eve believed what the Serpent said was true and followed his advice. Yes! Yes! She did!"

"What about Adam," Bobby asked, "did he also believe the lies?"

"No! Oh my! No! Adam was never fooled by the Serpent. When he took the fruit from Eve and ate, he knew it was wrong. He only ate it because Eve had, and he wanted to share all her experiences. Yes! Yes! He did! And I believe he had just a hint of desire within to want to be his own boss. A desire to make decisions and take actions without consulting anyone, including The Creator! If he had chosen not to eat, Eve would have eventually come to realize the Serpent lied to her and would have completely recovered. Yes! Yes! She would! But now the process of death has begun in both of them. The pure life placed in Adam by The Creator would have staved off the death that entered when Eve ate the forbidden fruit. But he, too, ate and now everything must change. Yes! Yes! It must!"

"I know some kids at school who smoke," Sally said, "even though they know it's not good for them. They think it's smart because the bigger kids, or someone they idolize, smokes. I bet they won't think it's smart when their parents find out. Was that how Adam felt?"

"Yes! Yes! Something like that. Perhaps! Yes!"

"What's going to change?" Bobby asked.

"You've already seen evidence of change. Yes! You have!"

"Do you mean the glow that vanished from around Adam and Eve?"

"Yes! Yes! Of course! That's only one small indication of many changes that will affect the entire Garden -- the entire earth -- and all living on it."

"Gabby, I still don't understand. What else will change?"

"Oh! Dear me! You always do ask the most difficult questions. I'll try my best! Yes! I will! Let me see. How can I explain? Yes! That's it! All plants need sunlight or they would surely die. Oh! Dear me! Die -- how I hate that word, particularly at this time! Explain what's going to change! Yes! Explain! In order to survive, all life needs energy from the sun. Yes! But for life to survive in the Land of the Beginning, another kind of energy is needed. I don't know what to call it! Let's just say it's an energy, a grace from the Son, a favor from The Creator, a gift from God. In your world, grace restores a person's relationship with God. Here, grace is the power that flows from The Creator, holding back death and decay. Yes! Yes! Grace is the power! Adam and Eve were the chosen channels of the power of His grace to every creature. Somehow, when they disobeyed and ate the fruit, their action blocked this power. If Adam hadn't eaten, the light of God's grace would still be flowing through him and Eve. Yes! Yes! It would! But Bobby, as you saw, the light of this power was snuffed out."

"You mentioned dying," Sally said. "Will Adam and Eve die?"

"Oh! Dear me! I don't know how to explain! No! I don't! Let me think! Dying in the Land of the Beginning takes longer than in your world. Adam and Eve will live for hundreds of years. But yes, their dying has already started. Oh! Dear me! Yes! It has! Do you know the real meaning of death?" Gabby paused, then answered his own question. "Death means separation. Adam and Eve have lost their intimate relationship with The Creator -- a separation has occurred. It's not because He has changed. Oh! My! No! He never changes! But they have, and never again will they feel comfortable before Him. You shall see! Yes! Yes!"

"Then why did I feel so comfortable, so safe, and so secure when I was with The Lamb or Lion?"

"Dear me! Can't you ask an easy question? But then, truth always does contain hard questions. Yes! Let me see! You're still responding to God as if you were in your own time. You're seeking the sacrifice of The Lamb -- of God, Himself. Yes! You are! But I'll explain more about that later; it's in the Book! Yes! It is! A comfortable relationship with The Creator can only be restored by accepting His favor."

"What do you have to do to be restored?" Bobby asked. "How can we accept His favor and continue in the wonderful relationship we've had with Him here?"

"Simply by believing and trusting in what He's done. Later in earth's history, God will come to the world as a man, the Lord Jesus Christ. And He will die! Because of this, we will never have to spiritually die or be separated from Him. No! Never be separated from Him! Trusting Him means you must be willing to obey Him. Yes! Yes! It does!"

"I want to trust Him," Sally said.

"Me too!" Bobby echoed.

Gabby beamed. "Trusting The Creator is the most important part of truth. Trusting Him is the beginning of all truth. Your journey here has been worthwhile if you remember those words. Yes! At the proper time you will know what He wants of you. Remember, in your world His power remains unchanged, and, if you truly desire to follow Him, He will give you the strength to do so. Yes! Yes! He will!"

"What's going to happen to the animals? Will they become dumb and uninteresting like they are back home?" Bobby asked.

"Yes! But the process will take time. Yes! It will! Adam and Eve protected them so the Evil One couldn't approach them. Now that wall of protection is gone, and he will coerce many into following his evil ways. But it's going to take a long time because cooperation between the animals will gradually break down. Bees will continue working together to gather honey and beavers will still build dams; but, never again, will you see a dog working with a horse, or a cat with a mouse. No! No! You won't! A few animals will remember Adam's kingship and, in a limited way, continue to work with man. But many will come to fear man; others will become man's enemy."

"Gabby, can we still treat the animals in the Garden the same?" Bobby asked.

"No! Oh my! No! You'll have to be very cautious. No longer can you predict how they'll react or behave. But there's no real danger. No! No danger!"

"Will Bobby and I be affected by what Adam and Eve did?"

"Every living thing will be affected and -- you're alive -- aren't you? Yes! Yes! You're alive," he said laughingly. But then he grew serious. "Here in the Garden, the character flaws you brought with you from your world have been covered. But now those flaws will reappear. In the next few days, you'll probably become irritated with one another. Yes! Yes! At times, you will! In fact, if you're not careful, you may get into a minor scrap or maybe even a major disagreement. Remember though, you're living in the Garden and you know The Creator. You can always go to Him for help and He'll be there. Yes! Yes! He's always there! Be constantly on guard and try to control your behavior. Enough talk! We have to go! Yes! We do! Important events are taking place which you should see and hear. Listen!"

In the distance, they heard a familiar voice. It was the majestic voice of The Father of Lights, the voice of The Lion of the Tribe of Judah, the voice of The Lamb. And it was coming closer, coming through the rooms of the Garden -- coming and calling -- calling: "Adam, where are you? Adam, where are you? Adam . . . "

CHAPTER TWENTY

As they started to leave, Sally asked, "Doesn't The Creator know where Adam and Eve are?"

"He knows," was Gabby's terse reply.

"Then why is He calling them?"

"Adam and Eve realize that what they did was wrong, and they have to face The Creator. In any healing that is the first step. But the healing won't be easy. Oh! No! It certainly won't!"

The Creator's voice drew closer and closer. His voice was so clear that for a moment they thought He had entered the room. They could hear Him calling, but the only thing they saw was a vague shimmering in the air as He passed. "Come! Quickly!" said Gabby, as he began to follow the shimmering air. The children joined him, following the voice which was calling Adam and Eve -- calling with such love and compassion. They didn't understand how Adam and Eve could resist responding. The voice in the shimmering air moved into the Command Room so quickly that they had to hurry to keep up.

"Adam! Eve! Where are you?"

This time they heard a faint response -- almost a whisper -- come from behind a hedge at the far end of the room. It was Adam. "We heard you calling us but we were cold and naked and afraid to answer. Eve used some fig leaves to make us clothes."

"Who told you that you were unclothed and naked? Adam, have you eaten fruit from the Tree of Knowledge of Good and Evil? Eaten that which I specifically commanded you not to eat? It is not the lack of clothing that causes your fear. You fear because in your heart you know you have rejected My wisdom and protection. You fear because you are now walking into uncertainty, into the unknown, into a death which separates you from Me. You feel exposed, not only on the outside, but also on the inside."

Eve sheepishly emerged from her hiding place to join Adam. Seeing them, Sally was surprised, not because their glow was gone -- she expected that -- but by their clothing. Eve, with skillful fingers, had sown fig leaves into multicolored garments and, although she used fresh leaves, they already looked faded and worn. They no longer looked as they did when Sally picked them for her. "Gabby, what happened to the leaves? Yesterday they were fresh and smooth as leather -- now they look old and fragile!"

"Remember when I told you Adam and Eve were channels. Well, the channel of The Creator's blessing through them is now closed, but the energy flowing through the channel to nature hasn't been completely blocked. At least, not yet! No! No! Not yet! That means energy can still flow both ways through the channel -- to Adam and Eve -- and away from them. Their bodies, in an attempt to keep warm, are literally pulling vitality out of the leaves causing them to decay."

"It looks like Eve used old autumn leaves," Bobby said. "It doesn't look like their clothing will last much longer."

"You shall see. Yes! Yes! You will! Be quiet! Listen! You need to hear what they're saying. In order for you to know why your world is the way it is, you need to know what happened in the beginning."

For a long time Adam and Eve stood silently in the presence of the shimmering air, before their Creator. Finally Adam spoke, "The woman you gave me -- Eve -- it's really her fault. She's the one who gave me the fruit and, following her example, I ate it." Sally watched Eve give Adam a look of pure displeasure. It was the first time Sally had seen her frown.

The Creator's voice penetrated like a knife. "Didn't I give you a mind of your own to uphold the truth, uphold the right? What is this that you have done?"

"It's... It's not like Adam says," Eve replied in a faltering voice. "It wasn't my fault; it was the Serpent's. He told me the fruit was good and I believed him."

"Eve, why did you listen to him and not Me? You know I always speak the truth. And I clearly told you that if you ate that fruit, it would bring death to the Garden."

"When I looked at the fruit, it seemed so right to eat. It was beautiful, unblemished, and smelled so good. And, when I tasted it, the flavor was delicious." Sadly she continued, "Isn't there a way back? I feel so empty -- so cold." She shivered.

"Eve, there is no way back -- you can only go forward. And the road ahead will not be easy -- for Me -- or for you." Looking around the Garden, His voice suddenly grew harsh. "I see you Serpent and I know the evil in your heart."

The children were surprised. They had not noticed the Serpent when they first entered the room. But there he was -- sulking in the far corner! The Creator continued speaking, "Because of the wickedness and pride in your heart, you became the source of Eve's temptation:

Cursed are you above all the beasts of the field,

Against them you will not your clever tongue wield.

But as a punishment for this, your heinous deed

As the cattle on grass and shrub you shall not feed,

But on your stomach in the dust you shall be made to crawl

Forced to look up at all other beasts both large and small.

Between you and the woman there shall be endless hate,

But this is just the beginning of your ultimate fate;

For your offspring and the woman's will remain enemies

Until the day the woman's Son will gain lasting victory.

In your bitterness you will be able to bruise His heel

As your head is crushed and He, His triumph seals."

As The Creator spoke, Bobby watched the Serpent's hind legs start to shrink. They continued to shrivel until he could no longer sit upright and toppled over. Like a giant lizard, he slithered away. Bobby noticed his once large legs were now so small he could barely see them.

Sally, watching the Serpent slither into a hedge, shuddered as she thought, *He looks just like a giant snake. I've always hated snakes and now I know why!*

The Creator spoke. This time in a kinder and gentler tone. "Eve, you will have to bear the consequences of your actions.

Your sorrow and trials will be greatly multiplied

Because my commands you ignored, you unthinkingly defied.

In pain and discomfort you your own children shall bear

But a greater burden shall be their nurture, their care;

You shall have more children than you can handle with ease

Till from the never ending task you will cry for relief.

And in everything you do, you will have to ask permission

Due to your sin, Adam over you the rule has been given."

Again he paused, "Adam, because you listened to Eve when you knew what she was asking you to do was wrong; you, too, will suffer. And, unfortunately, the world with you.

Because of your own actions and for your own sake,

The ease of living I from you will now take;

A curse I have placed on all parts of the ground

No longer on earth will food in abundance be found.

Heartaches, toils and trials will be your constant lot,

For plants will not bring forth fruit as they ought

But the earth will bring forth thorns and thistles instead

Until in your toil you despair of ever getting ahead.

The sweat of your brow and the ache of your back

Will alone be between you, yours, and serious lack --

Until the day to the dust of the ground you return

This the fate your disobedience has for you now earned.

"Adam, I say to you, remember the things which I have told you. Remember that eventually, in the future, there will be victory in the Son.
Your clothing will soon wear out and fall off. Only my grace can cover the hurts inside you. But, for now, I will do something practical and cover you on the outside with more durable clothing. Learn from what I do. The only thing that can cover death is life -- My life." He spoke the last sentence so softly and with such sorrow that for a moment Sally thought she had imagined the words. Then He

continued with words that sounded far away. "I bring a substitute." The shimmer in the air disappeared.

While The Creator was speaking, Adam and Eve had remained silent. Now Eve spoke, "Adam, what are we going to do?"

"From now on I intend to do the intelligent thing and obey The Creator. I don't know how well we'll succeed or what we'll have, but we won't be alone -- I'll have you and you'll have me. Who knows, maybe it won't be too bad. One thing I'm sure of is that things will never be the way they were. They'll never be the same," he repeated soberly. "Eve, this morning I called Hoppy and he ran from me and hid."

A moment later, two white coats made of sheepskin without blemish or spot fell at their feet. The shimmer in the air had returned. "Adam and Eve you are now covered by the sacrifice of another. Remember this -- I am still the One who provides your every need. The coats I have given you are thick, but they need to be if you are to keep warm. The warm glow you used to wear is gone and will never return. Write down what I have told you so in the days ahead, you'll remember. Soon I shall leave you and you will never see Me again face to face on this earth. But know this: I will see and hear you and will always be with you. You can call on Me. I answer those who do My will. Do you have any questions?"

After a short silence, Adam asked, "Can we still live in the Garden?"

"No! Never!" was the emphatic reply. "That would cause a horrible disaster. You must leave the Garden immediately. Because of my judgement, the Serpent's appearance has changed -- but his heart hasn't. And you have already proven that you are no match for him. If you stay in the Garden, he will try to trick you into eating fruit from the Tree of Life. And, if he succeeded, you would become like him -- unable to die -- eternally bound in corruption. Part of your punishment for disobedience is death, but death doesn't have to be final. I have created it to be an escape hatch that can be the pathway to a new life for you, your children, and your children's children. And, even though that new life is reached through death, it extends beyond death. I have spoken. Hurry now. Leave the Garden. Don't look back. Changes have already started. Soon I will block the ways in and out of the Garden."

The children heard a distant rumble and the ground shook slightly. "Gabby, do we have to leave, too?" Bobby asked.

"Yes! Yes! Of course! From this time on, there will be nothing to see in the Garden except decay. There's nothing more for you to see or learn. No! No! There isn't! You heard The Creator -- there are things worse than dying. To stay here would be just as dangerous for you as it is for Adam and Eve. They are not safe from the Evil One and neither are you. Yes! Yes! We must leave! And soon! Now!"

They followed Adam and Eve as they slowly walked out of the Garden.

CHAPTER TWENTY ONE

As Gabby and the children walked out of the Garden, they heard loud rumblings, immediately followed by a violent shaking of the earth -- earthquakes! At times the shaking was so violent and so intense that they were almost thrown to the ground. Because it was difficult to hear, they walked in silence. But they didn't mind not speaking since everyone was in a solemn mood. Finally, Bobby shouted loud enough to be heard. "I hate to walk when the ground is shaking like this -- it's almost impossible. Gabby, I know the Garden is losing its beauty but I still don't understand why we couldn't stay. I felt so safe there. I know I'll feel better when we find another safe place. Tell me, if The Creator can do anything He wants and didn't want Adam and Eve to eat from the Tree of Life, why didn't He just move the tree to another continent?"

"The Creator always does what is wise. Yes! Yes! He does! And don't forget that in the Land of the Beginning there is only one continent. Moving the tree to another location wouldn't take it out of the reach of man. Oh! No! Indeed it wouldn't!"

"Then maybe He should destroy the tree," Bobby suggested. "What purpose does it serve? Is it needed to sustain life? You haven't told us much about it -- except that it grows wherever The Creator makes His home. He isn't going to live in the Garden anymore, is He? I'm sure the tree doesn't grow in our world, so I'm not sure why its existence is necessary."

"The Tree of Life is needed for life in this time. Later, if He chooses to do so, The Creator may answer your questions. But the tree isn't the only danger in the Garden. Oh! Dear me! No! Absolutely not! Explanations again! Oh! I hate to explain! Especially when I don't know the best way to start. Let me think... Power! Yes!

That's it! Power! In your world men are only now beginning to discover the power locked within an atom. And the power in a single atom is only a small portion of the power in the universe. Power by itself is neither good nor bad. No! No! It isn't! But when it's used for evil, it's extremely dangerous. Of course, it can also be used for good. In the Garden there was a great power, a good power, which permitted everything to run smoothly. Now that evil has entered, the good power is being twisted into evil. Yes! The Garden is no longer safe. Since there was a great power of good there, great evil is now possible. Evil too great for you to handle."

"Gabby, are the earthquakes a part of the evil power being released?" Bobby asked.

"Oh! Dear me! No! Not really! The Creator is using earthquakes to rearrange the landscape and block off the Garden, isolating it so the animals will never be able to return to this dangerous place."

Bobby was curious. "How is he doing that?"

"If you're asking what power The Creator is using, the answer is-- I don't know -- only He knows. If you're asking what changes He's making to seal the Garden, I can tell you since I have also lived in the new world He's creating. To the West, the ocean has started to expand and will soon lap against the newly created shores of the Garden's western border. To the South, He's shutting off the streams that supply water to the land. He's also diverted the mist that provided night moisture to the plants. Yes! Yes! He has! Soon the Garden will be bordered by an extremely desolate and barren band of desert. To the North, the marshes and hot springs in the *Uncertain Wastelands* have expanded, making travel extremely difficult, if not impossible. It's much worse now than when we traveled through it because He has added large areas of quicksand between the hot pools. Yes! Yes! He has! In the East, -- well, you shall see that shortly."

As soon as Gabby stopped, Bobby asked, "Where is the Garden located in our world? I know it's no longer there but what land was it in? Over the centuries, the map of the world has changed so much that no one knows exactly where the Garden was."

"I'll only tell you this. The Creator loves the Garden, not only here in the Land of the Beginning, but also in your time. Remember, it's a land He loves. Yes! Yes! He does! If you study, you'll understand what I'm saying."

"Bobby, how about giving me a chance to ask a question! I want to know more about what The Creator said to Adam and Eve."

"Sally, you had your chance to talk earlier but were too busy looking around."

"That's not so; earlier it was too noisy. Now that the earth has stopped shaking, it's quiet. Besides, I've been so overwhelmed by everything that's happened, I didn't know where to begin. And now that it's quiet and I want to talk, you're not giving me a chance."

As she spoke, Sally harshly struck the ground twice with her tail and stuck out her tongue at Bobby. He laughed. Anyone seeing a huge Tyrannosaurus stick out its tongue would understand why he laughed. At first Sally looked indignant; then joined him in laughter. Their quarrel was over almost before it had begun. "Bobby, I'm serious, I really do have important questions."

"What is it you want to know?" Gabby asked. "I don't know the answers to everything but I do try to do my best. Yes! Yes! I do!"

"From now on will Eve be completely unhappy and sad?"

"No! She'll still have much happiness! Remember, The Creator told her He would always be with her, so in some ways she's still covered by Him. But, yes! Indeed yes! Her sorrows will grow and be hard to bear and she'll have many disappointments. Yes! She will! And Adam, too!"

"How many children will she have?"

"You do have important questions, don't you? I'll just say she'll have lots and lots. More than enough to keep her and Adam from being lonely! Yes!"

"I'm still not done," Sally said, seeing Bobby glance in her direction as if he had something to say. "What about Adam, will things be difficult for him? Will he be able to work hard enough to feed his family?"

"The evil that has entered the world still rests lightly on Adam. Yes! His character matches that of the greatest rulers in your world. So, if he works hard, he'll do well and his family will lack for nothing. No! They won't lack! But there are worse things..." He said this last sentence very softly.

"At church I've heard people talk about the Serpent and the Son of the woman. What were they talking about?"

"You should know. Yes! Yes! You should! In your world, it has already happened."

"Are they talking about the Christmas story, and other stories about Jesus? Some claim many of the stories are false -- that His disciples made them up to try and convince people how great a man Jesus was."

"Made up," Gabby snorted. "Made up! No! Indeed! The stories His disciples told are no more made up than this world we're walking on. And, I'm sure you've found this world to be very real. Yes! In fact, at this particular moment, perhaps too real. The Creator gave His Book to the world. Read it and you will find Jesus is called the second Adam. He's the One who will restore the world to what it was meant to be and make it even more glorious than the Garden."

"The Lion and The Lamb I saw . . . were they Jesus?"

"Now that's an easy question to answer. Yes! Of course!"

"The Lion looked so unhappy when he saw Eve eat the fruit. Was He sad because He knew He'd have to die on a cross because of what she did?"

"Yes! Of course! He knew He'd have to die. But that's not the reason He was sad. His unhappiness was caused by His thoughts of Adam and Eve and the heartache and sorrow they and their children would have to endure. He thought of sickness, death, cruelty and torture, of all the things that can and will go wrong in the world. He thought of many things -- but not the Cross. No! Oh! No! He wasn't sad, because the Cross is to be His glory. Yes! Yes! His glory! Only by the Cross can He create a way for Adam and Eve's children to escape death. He will die there for you, too. Yes, for you Sally and Bobby, because you are their distant children. It is through the Cross that He undoes sin and makes the world right for everyone who trusts Him. That is a truth which will never die. Remember it! Yes! Yes! Remember!"

Bobby wanted clarification. "Does trusting Him mean that we trust in what He's going to do . . . I mean in what He's done for us at Calvary?"

"You're right! Yes! Yes! You are! Just as He covered Adam and Eve with spotless coats, He also covers your every wrong and naughtiness. There is nothing He can't make spotless."

"I'm glad I've begun to trust Him and that Sally and I were allowed to come to the Garden. If I hadn't come here, I don't know if I ever would have listened to the truth. But," he admitted, "I still have a lot to learn. It's sad to watch something so beautiful being destroyed."

They came to the edge of the Garden where, not more than a week earlier, they had walked along the hedges forming the Garden's borders. Now the hedges had grown so large that they were difficult to recognize. Tightly woven together, they formed an impassable barrier -- a barrier covered with thick, long, thorns. None of the hedges in the Garden had had thorns before.

"I'm glad the gates are open and we don't have to go through the hedges," Sally exclaimed. "Those cruel thorns look positively wicked. And look, the dragons are here! But now they don't appear to be as friendly as they were before."

"Let's go," Gabby said as he hurried through the gate. "The dragons are here because they've been assigned to be guardians of the gate. Soon they won't allow anyone to pass in or out."

Following Gabby through the gate, Sally said, "I already feel better. Now that we've left the Garden, I don't feel as depressed."

"I agree! Yes! I do! Now that the earth has stopped shaking we can walk more easily. And that makes a difference in how we feel. Yes! It does!"

Until Gabby mentioned it, they hadn't realized the earth had stopped rumbling and how quiet it had become. Gabby continued, "You must never forget! No! Never! The world has been touched by evil and is no longer safe. No! No! It isn't! You must always be aware and keep your ears and eyes open. I suggest we head North -- until we reach the river. Away from the desert! We'll need to find food, water, and a safe shelter so we can rest. Yes! Yes! Need to rest! It's been an exhausting day."

Sally realized she, too, was exhausted -- so tired she found it difficult to put one foot in front of the other. "I hope we reach the river soon! Right now I'm so tired I don't care what it looks like."

CHAPTER TWENTY TWO

Even though she was exhausted, Sally didn't sleep well. They had finally stopped for the night in an orchard, taking shelter under a large apple tree. The tree they were under, and the trees around it, formed a sheltered nook which was out of sight of the path they'd taken into the orchard the night before. It wasn't the earth tremors that kept her awake; they were no longer strong enough to shake the ground. The primary reason she had difficulty sleeping was a scary, unexplained noise. Also thoughts of the events of the past two days raced in her mind! Every time she was about to fall asleep, she heard a soft thud. There would be silence -- then the thud again. Sometimes the thuds came close together with barely a pause in between.

From the moment she had lain down, she heard the sounds, making her wish she had a blanket to hide under. Just as she was about to wake Gabby to ask him about the noises, an apple fell on her head. This, of course, made her jump. But, after realizing that falling apples were the source of the mysterious sounds, she relaxed. Thinking about it, she chuckled. Here, the cause of her fear was the innocent sound of ripe apples falling to the ground! *At least I've learned something,* she thought. *Never again will I sleep under a fruit tree.* Closing her eyes, she continued to think. *Those sounds are nothing to be afraid of. Oh, I might get hit by another apple, but the last one didn't hurt and, if I'm hit again, it won't hurt me either.* She knew she was tense and had a sense of foreboding, of impending evil, which the sounds enhanced.

Finally, sleep came. But after what seemed only a moment, she opened her eyes to find bright sunlight streaming down through the tree branches. *I'm still sleepy,* she thought, *but it's already late.* The sense of foreboding was still with her and she shook her head trying to force it from her mind. She decided to join the others for breakfast.

"Breakfast sure isn't going to be a problem this morning," she said, raising herself up and seeing the ground carpeted with apples. "I'm surprised more of the apples didn't hit us. Or maybe they did and we were just too tired to notice."

"How long will it be before the apples start to rot? I wouldn't want them to go to waste," Bobby said as he scooped up two of them and chomped them down. "Right now they're delicious -- not spoiled at all!"

"Even in your world, apples last a long time after picking. And here, in this time after the... the fall, they last even longer. Yes! They do! Oh, yes! Perhaps ten times longer. Food that would spoil in three days will last a month here. For example, an apple which stays fresh for a month in your world will be edible for over a year in the Land of the Beginning. But the fruit on the ground won't last that long since many of the world's creatures don't know how to take care of it and will waste it. Yes! Yes! They will! They'll bite into it and that will hasten its spoilage. For awhile there will be more than enough food, but over the next year or so it will become scarce. Never again will the trees bring forth the crops you now see them yielding. No! Oh! No! Never again!"

After eating several more apples, Gabby suggested they get a drink from a nearby stream that was merrily bubbling through the orchard. *At least something sounds cheerful,* Sally thought.

"On our way we'll check the orchard for more food," Gabby said, leading the way to the stream.

The children followed closely. Just before reaching the stream, Sally froze in her tracks. There to her right, underneath a peach tree, she saw a pile of bloody feathers. She didn't want to think about what might have happened to the bird, but ugly unbidden thoughts pushed into her mind. *Had a bird been killed? Eaten?* She rushed to catch up with and be close to the others.

Arriving at the bank of the stream, she took a long drink of cool water. When Gabby and Bobby began eating the large strawberries that were growing there, she found she no longer had an appetite. When she didn't join them, Gabby asked, "What's wrong? Why aren't you eating?"

"Back in the orchard, I saw a pile of bloody feathers under a peach tree. Some bird, perhaps even our friend Whooty, was hurt there."

"Come! Take us back and show us where," Gabby said gravely.

Eager to investigate, Bobby excitedly said, "Let's go!"

Sally became angry, "All boys ever think about is adventure. You don't seen to care that perhaps one of our friends has been hurt or maybe even killed!"

He ignored her and trotted off toward the orchard.

"Wait for us," Gabby commanded. "For safety, we should stay together."

Bobby slowed down but still remained well ahead of them. Arriving at the peach tree first, he quickly spotted the scattered feathers and began looking for signs of what happened.

Gabby joined him in studying the feathers while Sally remained at least ten yards away. Trembling, she refused to go any closer or even look at the feathers.

"It looks like the Serpent has been here. Yes! Yes! It does!" Gabby said. "This looks like his work -- something he would do. Yes! This is his work!"

"Look!" Bobby exclaimed. "Someone stepped on one of the peaches." Pointing, he continued, "Whoever smashed it was going in that direction."

"Boys," Sally said disdainfully, "sometimes I just don't like boys!"

Ignoring her comments, Gabby shouted, "Bobby, wait! Wait for us -- don't get so far ahead!"

"Sally's slow and I can't wait all day," Bobby replied. "She's a girl -- a sissy!"

"I am not! It's just that I have a heart for others and you don't -- you don't care!"

Bobby pretended he didn't hear her. "It looks like there's a small ravine that goes to the stream. I'm going down," he called back as he ran into the ravine.

"Bobby -- stop!" Gabby shouted.

A moment later, when Bobby came face to face with the Serpent, they heard his startled, "Oh!" and watched in horror as the Serpent rushed toward him. As Bobby turned to flee, he saw the Serpent had no legs and was propelling his body forward by an undulating slithering motion. His head was topped with glittering diamonds and, as he hurled himself forward, his evil eyes were filled with hatred. With his mouth wide open, his teeth appeared longer and sharper -- like fangs maliciously dripping with poison. Bobby knew he had foolishly placed himself in danger. He had been showing off, partly because of Sally's remarks and also because -- well, he didn't quite know why. Although he was running as fast as he could, it felt as if he were under water, running in slow motion.

Gabby rushed past him, heading directly for the Serpent. "Keep running!" he shouted as he went by.

Bobby heard an evil hissing sound and then, behind him, the sound of body striking body.

"Now you've done it," Sally snarled as Bobby ran toward her. "What can we do to help Gabby? What will happen to us if he doesn't come back?" She had tears in her eyes.

"Come! Follow me! Let's return to the stream," Bobby said in a high squeaky voice as he ran past her. A few steps later, he reluctantly slowed to allow her to catch up.

"Shouldn't we go back and try to help?" Sally panted. Behind them they could clearly hear the sounds of battle -- the crashing and thrashing of bodies.

"Gabby told me to run. I think we should obey!"

"Now's a fine time for you to think about obeying. Why didn't you obey when he told you not to run ahead?"

Bobby was ashamed and, instead of answering, dejectedly hung his head. When they arrived at the stream, they saw a large lion. "I sure hope it's tame," Bobby muttered.

"Welcome, children! Fear not for I am with you."

"Oh, it's you! It's you!" Sally exclaimed. "The Lion of the Tribe of Judah. Can you do something to help Gabby?"

"Haven't you guessed! Gabby is My messenger. Nothing can harm him."

"Messenger?" Sally repeated, obviously puzzled.

"In your world my messengers are often called by other names."

"Angels?"

"Yes, angel is one of their names."

"But I thought angels had wings," Sally said

"Some do, but not all; it depends on the circumstances. But now, come with me." As The Lion spoke this command, the landscape darkened, totally blotting out all light. Suddenly, they were next to The Lion, looking down at the world of the beginning from the edge of a cloud. They were higher than a plane could fly -- higher than they had ever been before. It was like looking at the earth from outer space. Bobby recognized the continent below from the Command Room map. He thought it looked about the same as on the map except that the tongue of ocean running into the continent had greatly increased in size. *When we traveled with Adam and Gabby,* he thought, *we could only see a tiny part of the world. Now it appears our adventure in this world is over.*

"Will we be allowed to see the rest of the world -- the parts we didn't get a chance to explore?" Bobby asked.

"You are leaving and will never again be allowed to journey to the world of the Garden. You have both done well here; you have started to walk in My truth."

But Bobby was persistent. "Why can't we return?"

"Gabby brought you here to seek the truth. I am The Truth and The Life. After you have grown in truth -- in Me -- then we shall see about your returning."

"If Bobby's allowed to return, can I come, too?"

"Yes! And remember, truth is not only in knowing. It is also in doing! Both of you have doing hearts and have grown in doing. But there is even more growing and doing ahead. To know Me is to trust. Trust Me!"

Bobby blinked his eyes and, instantly, Sally, the Tyrannosaurus disappeared; Sally, the girl, was standing in her place. Looking down, he saw that he, too, was back in his old body. To be sure, he lifted his hands and looked at them. They looked as they always had, perfectly normal. Then, far below, he saw the continent of North America. It looked just like pictures he had seen which had been taken from space. They were back in their own world -- their own time. As The Lion's voice faded, they heard Him say, "Remember, walk in the truth!"

Once more the world darkened and became blurry. When Bobby focused his eyes, he found he was sitting beside Sally in the cloakroom outside of Mr. Meed's office. They were back at school! They were home!

CHAPTER TWENTY-THREE

Bobby looked around and shook his head. "What a strange dream! I must have fallen asleep."

"I'm not so sure," Sally replied. "In fact, I know you weren't having a dream. Because, if you were, I was in it. We were back..." Her sentence was disrupted by the opening of the principal's door.

"Bobby, you and Sally may come in now. I'm sorry to have kept you waiting so long. My last appointment took longer than expected. As you probably know, some of the children don't like to wait in this room. They think it's spooky."

As they entered his office, Mr. Meed shut the door. "Bobby, Miss Little has told me she's concerned about your behavior. It sounds like most of the day you've been in a dream world of your own and haven't paid attention in class. That's not like you. Is something wrong?"

Bobby didn't know what to say. "No, I'm fine, nothing's wrong. It's just been a strange day. Usually I don't daydream -- really I don't. I don't know why I'm doing it today. I'm not sick and I slept good." He hesitated as he mentioned "*sleeping well*," because last night his sleep in "*the world after the fall*" had been troubled and restless. Sally's had, too. But, he was talking about his real home; his home in this world.

Sally chimed in, "Mr. Meed, while we were waiting we talked for quite a while. I didn't notice anything wrong with Bobby. He acted fine."

"I see you have an advocate," Mr. Meed smiled. "All right then, run along back to your class. You're certainly alert now. It's obvious whatever the problem was is now gone. Make sure you stay awake and pay attention. A fine mind like yours shouldn't be wasted daydreaming. If you're sent to me again ... next time I'll be stricter. Class is almost over for the day, scurry back and get your homework assignments."

As they left his office and entered the hallway, Bobby turned to look at Sally. "We really did go back to the Land of the Beginning, didn't we?" Then he added, "I know we did and that it was real, but it seems so impossible. If you hadn't been with me, I'd think it was just a vivid and strange dream."

"I have proof we were there. See!" she said, reaching into her purse and taking out a large red strawberry. I picked it today when we were by the stream and put it in my pouch." She wasn't sure if *"today"* was the correct word to describe something that had taken place thousands of years ago. "Remember when, after seeing the feathers, I didn't feel like eating. Well, just before we left, I picked this strawberry. It's real and real strawberries don't come from dreams."

Smiling, he said, "Sally, I, too, brought something back -- a friend! May I sit with you going home on the bus? I want to talk some more and, right now, we don't have time. We'd better be careful talking about Gabby and the rest. If the other kids hear, they'll think we're crazy. They'd probably believe that because you were sent with me to Mr. Meed's office, I somehow affected your mind. Maybe infected it with *'boy'* germs!"

She laughed. "You've found a friend and so have I! Of course you can share a seat with me on the bus." Quietly, they entered the classroom and returned to their seats.

Bobby's mind was racing, filled with the wonderful things that had happened, causing him to have difficulty concentrating during the few remaining minutes of class. But, by trying hard, he made it through without incident. *I bet Miss Little thinks I'm still dopey,* he thought. *I've only heard about half of what she said. I sure hope Sally can tell me what our homework assignment is. Thank goodness it's time for the bell.* Looking at Sally, he wasn't sure if she heard the homework assignment since she, too, seemed to be having difficulty concentrating.

At last class was over. The children rushed to put their books away and board the buses. The snow had melted but here and there in the coolness of a shady spot, patches of it still lingered. After putting her books away, Sally waited for Bobby so they could walk to the bus together. Near the front of the bus they found a vacant seat.

As they sat down, one of the children pointed at them and said, "Look, they're sitting together! I wonder what happened at the principal's office!" The other children laughed.

Bobby smiled as he thought, *You'd never guess what happened to us -- not in a million years.* Looking at Sally, he saw she, too, was smiling at their classmate's remark. "Let's not talk about *'you know what;'* there are too many ears listening. I'm glad we returned when we did. I mean, what would have happened if school had ended for the day and we weren't in the waiting room. They could have looked and looked but never would have found us. That sure would have caused a commotion. I do want the chance to talk about *'you know what.'* When can we get together?"

"We wouldn't have been late getting back. The Creator is the One who took us away and He controls everything -- including time." Then Sally answered his question, "If you want to, I'm sure it'll be all right for you to come over to my house this evening. My parents allow me to have friends over whenever I want."

"Sounds great, but I'll have to ask my parents. They're pretty neat though, so I'm sure they'll say it's okay. As far as I know, we don't have anything planned for tonight. If it were tomorrow, I couldn't come over. My dad's been real busy at work and tomorrow is special. He's taking me to the planetarium. I sure wish you could come with us. The stars would remind us of the beginning." Bobby was having difficulty keeping conversation away from the world which was filling his thoughts. "Your house is the gray-blue ranch on Hobson Street, isn't it? Last week when we were on the way to the store, I saw you playing in the front yard."

"Yep! That's my house. Here, let me write out my phone number. Call me and let me know if you can come. Maybe you can help me with my math. I have difficulty with it and sure could use some help!"

The bus, packed with a full load of children, left the school yard. Bobby and Sally were so busy talking they didn't even notice the bus was moving. "I really don't know much about you," Bobby said. "Do you have brothers or sisters?"

"Two sisters, but no brothers. My older sister is in high school and thinks she knows everything, or at least more than I do. But, after today, I know some things about the world that she doesn't. Don't you agree?" Smiling, she added, "Beginning things!" Her mind, like Bobby's, kept returning to their shared adventure, but she continued on. "Then, there's Liz, my younger sister, who is only three. She's really cute with long, curly, blond hair and sparkling blue eyes."

"Like Eve."

"She's not as beautiful, but she's my sister and I love her."

"Have you lived here long?"

"Most of my life," Sally answered. "We lived in Texas for a while when I was a baby, but I was so little I don't remember much about it."

They were surprised by how quickly the bus reached their stop. It seemed as if they had just sat down and started to talk. They clamored off the bus and stood looking at one another. "Sally, we're not *new* friends; we're *old* friends. After all, we've been friends since the very beginning."

After saying goodbye, they separated and began to walk home. Bobby whistled as he went. *At least I whistle better as a boy than I did as a Tyrannosaurus,* he thought.

"My, aren't you the cheerful one," his mom said as he entered the house. "You must have had a good day." Although she was a working mother, she had made arrangements with her employer so she could be home when Bobby returned from school.

Excitedly he said, "I had a wonderful day. I made a new friend. Her name is Sally. Mom, if we aren't doing anything after supper, can I go to her house to work on our homework? She only lives on the next block. Can I?" He paused and looked pleadingly at his mom.

"Whoa! Slow down! Dad's working late and I don't have anything planned, so sure you can go." She was pleased to hear he had a new friend because, inwardly, ever since moving here, she had concerns about his adjustment at the new school. She gave him a big hug. "You can go if you do your chores -- and some of your homework -- before you leave."

"As soon as I call Sally to let her know I can come over, I'll get started on my chores," he said. "And I promise -- I'll hit the books."

Time seemed to crawl but, at last, it was suppertime and his work was finished. He practically gulped down his food and then hurried off to see Sally.

She and Liz, her baby sister, were playing in the front yard. "My parents aren't here," she said. "They went out for the evening so I'm babysitting Liz, but she won't be a bother. Susie, my older sister, is up in her room with a large stack of homework so you probably won't see her."

Taking his hand, she led him into the house. "Before we can visit, I have to finish washing the dishes. I've done most of my homework except for math. Later, we can work on that together. While I finish the dishes, Liz can entertain you. Or rather, I should say, she'll gladly let you entertain her."

At first, when Sally took his hand, he felt shy and awkward. It had been a long time since he had had a really close friend. And now, he not only had a close friend -- he had a girlfriend. Liz soon put an end to his discomfort by taking his other hand and pulling him into the family room. Before long she had charmed him into reading her favorite stories. A short time later, Sally finished the dishes and joined them.

"What did you do with the strawberry?" he asked.

"I brought it home in my purse, and put it in the refrigerator right away. We can decide what we want to do with it later."

"It might be interesting to plant it and see if any strawberry plants would grow. But, even if plants did grow, I bet the berries wouldn't taste as good as the ones in the Land of the Beginning."

"What do you want to do first?" Sally asked. "Talk or homework?"

"Do you have a Bible? I'd like to read what it says about the beginning."

"We have one but haven't used it in ages. I think it might be on the living room bookshelf. Come, help me look." Liz followed them into the living room.

At first they had difficulty finding the Bible but finally located it on the top shelf. When he took it down, Bobby noticed it was covered with dust. He thought, *I bet from now on it won't gather dust.* Together they opened it to the first page and began to read, "In the beginning God created the heavens and the earth..." They read on.

"Those are the same words that were written in the Command Room," Bobby remarked.

"Hearing them, takes me back and makes me feel as though I were, once again, in the Garden."

"Wouldn't it be great if we could eat a custard acorn snack or go with Adam to visit the Sand Castle! Do you think The Creator will ever let us go back?"

"Not to the Garden as it was," Sally replied. "As the Lion of the Tribe of Judah, He was emphatically clear in telling us we could never return. But, He did hint that sometime we might go back to somewhere."

"If we do go back, I hope Gabby's our guide," Bobby told her. "He was a good friend and I miss him."

"I wonder if there's anything we can do to help us return?"

"I don't know if it will help us return but, if we read the Bible, I'm sure it wouldn't hurt. In fact, I think it would be fun to continue to read it together, don't you? If we study it, maybe we'll learn more about The Creator, creation, and our friends Adam and Eve. I want to learn everything I can about them. And also about Gabby, the angel messenger. I want to learn all I can about angels and so many other things."

"That's a great idea," Sally agreed, "let's set a time to get together every week."

"It would be nice if we could get someone to help us -- to guide us. I'm not sure how to begin. We need someone like Gabby."

"I'm sure that if we try, The Creator will be there to help us."

"Sally, you're right! Remember, He told us as long as we trusted in Him, He would be there for us."

For a moment they were silent, then Sally looked at Bobby and said. "When you were a Tyrannosaurus, you were bigger and somehow seemed more dignified."

"I agree with the bigger part. When you were a Tyrannosaurus, you looked older, more mature. I guess we were different because we were living in a world without sin. Sin is selfish and makes people childish. In our world we can't escape it. It's everywhere."

"What impressed you the most in the Land of the Beginning? What will you remember longest?"

"I'm not sure ... Not the beauty, though it was awesome. Not the food, though it was delicious and wonderful. I think the thing I'll remember longest is how everyone watched after one another and how they all worked together. Everyone was a friend to everyone else -- they acted like friends should. In the Garden we were bathed in true love and saw how The Creator meant the world to be."

Sally didn't like being serious for long. "Bobby, didn't this impress you?" she said, sticking out her tongue.

Remembering when she, as a Tyrannosaurus, stuck out her tongue at him, Bobby started to laugh . . . and then continued laughing . . . and laughing. Sally joined him.

"Why are you laughing?" Liz lisped, holding up her Raggedy Ann doll.

"When Sally gained control of herself, she winked at Bobby, and said to Liz, "Oh! Dear me! Explanations! How I hate explanations. Yes! Yes! I do! But, I'll do my best. Yes! Yes! I will!"